Better for Us

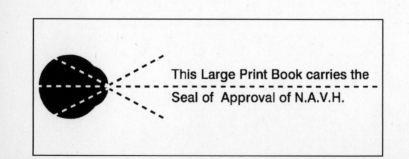

This Large Print Book carries the
Seal of Approval of N.A.V.H.

BETTER FOR US

VANESSA MILLER

THORNDIKE PRESS
A part of Gale, Cengage Learning

Detroit • New York • San Francisco • New Haven, Conn • Waterville, Maine • London

GALE
CENGAGE Learning®

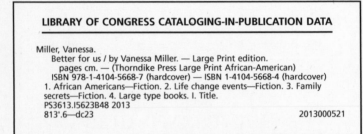

LIBRARY OF CONGRESS CATALOGING-IN-PUBLICATION DATA

Miller, Vanessa.
    Better for us / by Vanessa Miller. — Large Print edition.
      pages cm. — (Thorndike Press Large Print African-American)
    ISBN 978-1-4104-5668-7 (hardcover) — ISBN 1-4104-5668-4 (hardcover)
    1. African Americans—Fiction. 2. Life change events—Fiction. 3. Family secrets—Fiction. 4. Large type books. I. Title.
    PS3613.I5623B48 2013
    813'.6—dc23   2013000521

Published in 2013 by arrangement with Harlequin Books S.A.

For everyone who has loved, lost and
found the courage to love again.

CHAPTER 1

If Ryla Evans had known that by the day's end she would be running to her car and fleeing the scene, she would have worn flats rather than her skinny-heeled Jimmy Choos. Hobbling as she got into her car with one skinny heel in hand, she mumbled repeatedly, "Jimmy Choos are not for running," as her other heel just barely hung on. Ryla then quickly sat down, removed her other shoe and tearfully threw them both on the passenger side.

Fashionable, chic and *stylish* were words normally associated with Ryla Evans. She freely admitted that she loved shopping for clothes, shoes and purses. But she was a single mother, and had just left her corporate position to run her event-planning business full-time, so Ryla rarely bought anything that wasn't on sale. Her stilettos had been her one extravagance. But Noel Carter had ruined that enjoyment, just as he'd ruined her hopes and dreams almost eight years ago.

Tonight he'd had the audacity to strut his tall, dark and too-gorgeous self into the banquet hall as if the party was all about him. Ryla had been smiling as she handed a business card to a potential client, when she noticed the commotion going on over by the bar. The guy was a top-notch Houston attorney, just like tonight's guest of honor, and he didn't look like the kind of man who spent his time worrying about how much things cost . . . her favorite kind of client. Nearby, her ex-man and former NBA superstar Noel Carter was holding court, slapping hands, grinning and taking numbers as if he was still a wonder worker on the basketball court. Even though Noel's short-lived NBA career had ended three years ago, he was still sniffing on fresh air. She wasn't surprised. The lead dog in the pack always got the fresh air.

Stepping away from her potential client, Ryla made her way to the kitchen on the other side of the large banquet hall to speak with the chef. "How's everything going, Chef Michael?"

"Everything is superb, Ryla. Now what are you doing in my kitchen? You know I don't like lookie-loos in my kitchen."

Don Michael was too temperamental when it came to his kitchen. That was the one thing about him that got on her last nerve. But her clients always had extremely satisfied expressions upon their faces once they savored Don Michael's hors d'oeuvres. And with six out of ten of her clients asking for the chef's recipes, Ryla lived with his temperaments. "I was just checking to see if you needed my help with anything?"

"What? You don't have enough to do so you need to scrounge for work in the kitchen." His hand motions shooed her away. "Go, see to your guests up front and let me attend to my kitchen."

Ryla wanted to object. After all, she was the event planner, she had hired Don Michael and if she wanted to hide out in *his* kitchen, he couldn't do one thing about it. But Chef Michael was known not only for his exquisite hors d'oeuvres. He had walked off numerous jobs screaming bloody murder for the smallest of infractions. And his contract allowed him to keep two-thirds of the negotiated price whether he acted like a fool or not. So, Ryla wasn't going to mess with him. "All right, I'll just go on back out and check on my client."

With her head lowered, Ryla walked back toward the party wondering how in the world she could slip out without being noticed by Mr. Alpha Dog himself. But all that pondering came to an end as she crashed into an immovable force. Ryla stepped back. "I'm so s-sorry," she stammered as she stared into the deep, sultry brown eyes of Noel Carter.

"No need to apologize. I was looking for you."

"Uh, looking for me . . . Wh-why?" she asked, although Ryla knew exactly why Noel was looking for her. It was the same reason she had been trying to avoid him.

"I've been trying to find you ever since I saw you at that wedding reception last month."

Ryla had been thrilled when her best friend, Danetta Harris, and her longtime business partner, Marshall Windham, finally came to terms with their feelings for one another and got married. What she hadn't been so thrilled about was the fact Noel, an ex that she hadn't seen since college and hadn't bothered to tell about her pregnancy before breaking things off, had attended the reception with Marshall's cousin.

Jaylen had been with Ryla at the reception, and when Ryla locked eyes with Noel, she could tell that he was doing mathematical equations in his head, putting two and two together. So, she'd snuck Jaylen out of the reception and driven home as fast as she could. It wasn't that she never planned to see Noel again. Since leaving him the day she'd found him lip-locked with man-stealing Cathy O'Dell, Ryla knew that she would have to tell him about Jaylen one day. But with each passing year, the news became harder and harder to deliver.

"Can we have a seat for a moment? I need to speak with you about something." Noel tried to guide Ryla over to a pair of chairs in a dark little corner of the room.

"Sure, Noel, but give me a minute. I need to check with Jonathan to see if he needs anything," Ryla said softly, in an attempt to keep her cool. She then walked back toward the front of the room where the party was in full gear. Jonathan Conrad was celebrating becoming a partner in his law firm. And if the drinks and well wishes that had been floating around the room were any indication, his friends were delighted for him. They may have been more delighted that the drinks were on Jonathan, but Ryla wouldn't tell her client that.

Tapping Jonathan on the shoulder, Ryla put on a happy face as she said, "Things seem to be going well."

"Oh, Ryla, there you are. My buddy Noel

11

was looking for you a moment ago."

"I saw him," she answered and then got right back to business. "I just wanted to see if you needed anything."

Jonathan glanced around. "Nope, everything's moving smoothly. You weren't kidding about knowing how to throw a good party."

"It's my specialty." She looked over her shoulder to where Noel stood waiting for her to return. She then glanced at her watch as she turned back to Jonathan. "Look, if you don't need anything else, why don't I just get on out of here. I'll send a cleanup crew in about an hour and they'll clear everything out."

"That'll work. And hey, make sure you send a dozen or more of your business cards to my office. I'll hook you up with some more business."

"Thanks, Jonathan." Ryla backed away from her client, keeping an eye on Noel. She stood by the bar for a moment, pretending to be checking in with the bartender. The moment Noel took his eyes off her, Ryla quickly made her way to the side door. Once in the clear, she ran as if her life depended upon it.

Not so fast, Noel thought as he watched

12

Ryla make her escape. She had played this running game on him last month, when he'd seen her and that little girl at the reception. But Noel wasn't about to let her get away tonight without providing some answers. He took his keys out of his pocket and followed her out of the side door. Noel glanced around the parking lot, but didn't see Ryla anywhere. Standing next to his midnight-black Cadillac Escalade, he surveyed his surroundings. Then suddenly he saw a little red BMW pulling out of the parking lot as if the devil himself was after it.

Without pause, Noel swiftly jumped in his car and pursued the BMW. It looked like a car Ryla would drive . . . cute and compact. He kept a distance far enough behind to not alert her to the fact that he was in hot pursuit. Aside from the previous month, he hadn't seen Ryla Evans in almost eight years. Parts of him thought he should turn around and stop chasing after the only woman who'd ever managed to get close enough to break his heart. But he couldn't let her out of his sight now. Not when she had some explaining to do. Who was the little girl that had been with Ryla last month? And why had she called Ryla Mama?

He'd always wondered why Ryla had dropped out of college and dropped him as if he'd meant nothing to her. They'd made promises of love to each other and had promised to spend the rest of their lives together. All he'd asked Ryla to do was to wait until he graduated college and began his NBA career.

Late into the night, they had lain in each other's arms planning their lives together. Noel thought that Ryla had been happy with him. Noel had been happy . . . meeting Ryla had changed him. He had decided early on that he wasn't going to settle down with one woman until he was about thirty. He would then find a woman to marry who could give him a few kids. That very thought brought him back to the little girl he'd seen with Ryla. Had she been the reason Ryla'd left him?

He didn't have much time to ponder this, as Ryla pulled up to a brown-and-white duplex and jumped out of the car, carrying her shoes in her hand. "What in the world?" Noel said as he watched a barefooted Ryla make her way to the front door of one of the duplex houses, while stumbling on a few rocks as if she'd spent her night drinking rather than hosting a celebratory party.

Smiling to himself, Noel got out of his car

and followed Ryla's path. As he passed by her BMW, he caught a glimpse of the rust, dents and dings and realized that the car had to be at least a decade old. He lifted his hand to knock on her front door, and it swung open. She now had on a pair of pink tennis shoes with sparkly shoestrings, but was still holding one of the shoes she had worn tonight in her hand.

Her eyes popped out of her head as she was obviously shocked to see him standing there on her porch. She lifted the shoe in her hand and screamed at him, "You ruined my Jimmy Choos."

"What are you talking about?" Noel was totally caught off guard by Ryla screaming at him, when he was the one who had to act like a stalker to get a moment with her.

"Get out of my way. I think I have some superglue in my glove compartment." She shoved by him and stomped down her two-step porch.

Noel walked into the small duplex, sat down on the couch and got comfortable as if his name was on the deed. After fumbling around in her glove compartment, Ryla came back into the house, mumbling about hard-earned money.

"Are you all right?" Noel asked as he watched her struggle with the tube of superglue.

"Do I look all right?"

Noel stood, took the superglue out of her hands and opened it. He handed it back to her and then sat down again. "Why on earth do you keep superglue in your car?"

"I don't have the newest model car, if you haven't noticed." She shrugged. "Sometimes I have to glue things back in place."

"Why are you out buying Jimmy Choos if you can't afford to get a new car?"

"Hey, I saved for months to get these shoes. And I *choose* not to get a new car, because I'm putting the money into my new business . . . if it's any of your business." Ryla sat down and began to glue her shoe back together, as she asked, "And anyway, do you know that it's against the law to stalk a person."

"If I'm a stalker, then you must be crazy, because you left your front door wide open so I could walk in."

"Why did you follow me home? Isn't it obvious that I don't want to talk to you?"

Noel leaned back against the cushion of the couch. "Oh, it was obvious. But I've been trying to find you ever since I saw you at that wedding last month, because I definitely want to talk to you."

"Why don't you just talk to your little

girlfriend? The two of you seemed to be having a good time."

"Marla is not my girlfriend, as you put it. She and I are friends and I simply escorted her to her cousin's wedding. But that has nothing to do with what I need to speak with you about," Noel said pointedly.

Ryla kept her head down, continuing to press the heel to the base of the shoe.

He could tell that she was trying to avoid eye contact with him. That was all right with Noel, because as long as she wasn't looking at him, he was able to stare at her. And Noel liked what he saw . . . aside from the shoulder-length hair, Ryla hadn't changed in the past eight years. She was still beauty queen fine to him. He wanted to go to her, put his arms around her and remind her of their sweet yesterdays. But he wasn't here for that. "You don't want to know why I've been trying to find you?"

Ryla lifted her head. But she still didn't make eye contact. "I'm sure you're going to tell me."

"First I'd like for you to tell me something."

"What?" she asked, with suspicion lacing her words.

"Where's the little girl I saw you with last month?"

17

She placed her shoe and the glue on the coffee table as she nervously fidgeted with her hands, trying to remove the excess glue and stall for as long as possible. When she noticed that Noel seemed perfectly comfortable sitting on her couch waiting for an answer, she said, "She's not here."

"Where is she?"

"Why do you want to know?"

Getting irritated by their unproductive conversation, Noel shifted in his seat. "Since that question is too hard for you, let me ask another."

She nodded, giving him the go-ahead.

"Did you leave me when we were in college because you were pregnant with another man's baby?"

CHAPTER 2

No, he didn't just accuse her of cheating on him. "Come again?" she said with hands on hips.

He stood up and walked over to her. "You might need to get your ears checked, since you seem to be having a lot of trouble hearing me tonight."

Ryla's eyes traveled the distance as she gazed up at Noel. He was almost seven feet. When they were dating, Ryla was thankful for Noel's height, because at five-nine she'd dated a few guys who were shorter than her, and had always felt a little awkward. Today, rather than being a comfort to her, his height was more imposing than it had ever been.

She stood up, trying to get on equal footing with him, but even that made her feel a bit ridiculous since Noel was a full foot taller than her. "There's nothing wrong with my hearing — I just don't appreciate being called a cheater."

"Well, what am I supposed to think, Ryla?" Giving her a questioning glare, he asked, "Did you adopt that little girl I saw you with?"

With her arms folded she said, "No."

He clenched his fists as he turned away from her. Exhaling a burst of hot air, he whirled back around. "Why didn't you just tell me that you had a new man? Why'd you have to sneak out of my life like that without letting me know what was going on?"

Ryla rolled her eyes. She wished Noel wasn't so tall, because she really wanted to box his ears. How dare he assume that she was the kind of woman who would sleep with multiple partners. She wasn't the cheater — he was. "I see you're still a big dumb jock."

"Oh, I was never a big dumb anything." Then as he gave her a sinister grin he added, "Except when it came to you."

Ryla stomped her foot like a two-year-old and rolled her eyes. "She's yours, Noel. I'm not a cheater like *some* people I know!"

Noel looked around the room as if the little girl would suddenly materialize so he could verify Ryla's statement. "Did I hear you right?" His voice thundered as he turned back to Ryla.

Recognizing the fury in his voice, Ryla stepped back. She hadn't intended to just throw it out there like that. But Noel had made her mad when he accused her of cheating on him. She lifted her hands. "Noel, there's no sense getting all mad. Sit down and let's discuss this like two reasonable adults," she said, attempting to take control of the current situation.

He looked at her as if she was a known crackhead asking him for some spare change. "Oh, now you want to be reasonable. Well, I need to speak with my attorney first, and then I'll let you know just how reasonable I'm going to be." He moved away from her and headed toward the door.

But Ryla knew that an angry Noel could be a formidable opponent. She had once witnessed him losing badly to a team that was much better than his on the court. But during the third quarter, two of the players started taunting him and Noel got mad. Nothing but net was happening after that. The game might have sent Noel and his teammates to the locker room hanging their heads in shame, but because Noel refused to lose, that game ended up making him a star.

Ryla grabbed his arm as she implored him to stay. "Please, Noel, don't leave like this.

21

She'll be home tomorrow. Why don't you just come back over in the afternoon and I'll introduce you."

He shook her off his arm. "Do you even hear how you sound? You'll introduce me to my own child. . . . What kind of sense does that make, Ryla?"

She held up her hands in surrender. "Okay, you're right. I admit that this doesn't make much sense at all. But Noel, it's all we have. Now, I'm sorry that all of this is being thrown at you at once, but we don't need to get lawyers involved."

Noel laughed. But it wasn't a ha-ha kind of laugh. "You have kept a child from me for seven, eight . . . How old is she?"

"Seven. She'll be eight in July."

He shook his head. "You've kept a child from me for almost eight years and you've run from me each time I've seen you, but you expect me to trust you?"

"If you can't trust me, who can you trust?" Ryla deadpanned, as she did whenever she was backed into a corner with no escape. But as usual, the jokes didn't work for her.

"I'd rather trust a DNA test and my lawyer, if you don't mind?"

With a lifted brow, Ryla asked, "What do you need a DNA test for? Can't you count?

22

I just told you that her birthday is in July, so that should tell you that I got pregnant in October, during the fall."

"How do I know that you didn't get pregnant during Thanksgiving or Christmas break when you were home with your mom and her many boyfriends?"

Ryla jumped as if she'd been slapped. Noel had always been a daunting opponent, but she'd never known him to be outright mean. She'd heard all the reports about his gambling, drinking and womanizing during his NBA superstar days. Maybe all of that superstardom had gone to his head and turned him into someone she didn't know anymore. "Okay, if you want a DNA test, then we'll do that. But can we please just work this out between the two of us?"

"There's no longer just the two of us. We now have a daughter and I don't even know her name." Another laugh escaped his lips as he shook his head.

"It's Jaylen."

He swung back around and glared at Ryla. "You actually gave her my middle name and couldn't even pick up a phone to tell me about her?"

"Turn the page already," she said, and then slapped her hand across her mouth as she realized she was doing her deadpan thing, which never worked with Noel. She was just so nervous, even though she'd had seven years to prepare for this moment. She could have never been prepared for the challenge.

Ryla knew of a woman who tried to keep her children away from her ex-husband once they divorced. The judge didn't like what she was doing. So he awarded the cheating ex-husband full custody of the kids. Ryla in no way wanted lawyers and judges involved in this situation. She took her hands away from her mouth and pleaded. "I'm so sorry for saying that. But please listen to me. Jaylen wants to meet you. She's been asking me about her father for nearly a year now. But how do you think she will feel if she knows that her parents are fighting over her?"

Noel backed down a bit. "So you're saying that you won't run again?"

She nodded.

"And I can see Jaylen tomorrow?"

She crossed her heart and lifted a hand as if she was preparing to lay it on a stack of Bibles. "You have my word."

"And when can we get the DNA test done?" Noel asked, sounding all business.

Ryla's hands went back to her hips. "Are you really going to put Jaylen through something like that?"

"Hold on. Let's get something straight. I'm not putting Jaylen through anything." He pointed at Ryla. "You have put her through seven years of not knowing who her father is —"

"She knows who you are. I've shown her pictures of you countless times. She keeps a photo of me and you on her nightstand."

Noel grabbed his head and massaged his temples. When he looked at Ryla again, he said, "I don't know what made you do something like this, but I'm telling you now, if Jaylen is my child, I'll never forgive you for this." With that, he stormed out of her house.

Ryla plopped down on her couch, angry and spoiling for a fight herself. But the more she thought about it, the more she realized that she had already lost this fight. And it hadn't even begun yet. Noel had all the cards in his hand. He was rich and could afford the best lawyer that money and celebrity could buy. She, on the other hand, was a struggling entrepreneur with nothing but debt and a growing client list.

She had, however, just thrown a wonderful party for Jonathan Conrad, who was now a partner in one of Houston's top-notch law firms. He just might be willing to assist her with a pro bono attorney. Before she could begin to smile about her prospects, Ryla remembered that Jonathan was Noel's frat brother and would probably have more allegiance to his frat than to a business associate. Nevertheless she got on the phone and called the cleanup crew to ensure that they would take extra care with his cleanup. It never hurt to put the best foot forward. Because for all she knew, Noel and Jonathan might not be all that close anymore.

After hanging up with the cleanup crew, she dialed her best friend, Danetta Windham. Danetta was still a newlywed. Ryla figured that calling her at ten at night was surely going to annoy Marshall. But she couldn't worry about that right now. She needed help.

The phone rang four times before a giggling Danetta picked up. "Hey, Ryla, what's up?"

When she heard her friend's voice, it was as if a dam broke and tears began flowing down her lovely face. "I — I'm sorry to bother you so late, Danetta."

The laughter left Danetta's voice. "Are you all right, Ryla? It sounds like you're crying."

"Noel wants to get an attorney and he

wants a DNA test."

"Whoa, hold up. Are you talking about Jaylen's father?"

"Y-yes."

"When did all of this happen? The last I knew, you still hadn't spoken to him."

Wiping tears from her face, Ryla said, "All of that changed tonight. I ran into him at the party I was hosting for one of his frat brothers. And then he followed me home."

"You invited him back to your house after the event?"

Ryla frowned into the phone as if her friend wasn't keeping up, and she needed to be moving much faster than this. "No, of course I didn't. I tried to run from him again, but he followed me and then forced his way into my house. And now he's threatening me with lawyers and a DNA test. I still can't believe he wants a DNA test. Can you believe that?" Ryla was speaking fast, but not fast enough not to notice that Danetta hadn't responded to her question.

"Danetta, did you hear me?"

"Which part, hon. I'm trying to wrap my mind around all of what you've been telling me," Danetta said.

"About the DNA test. He claims that I could have gotten pregnant when I went home for Thanksgiving or Christmas break."

27

"Well, Ryla, you did expect this, didn't you?"

"No, I didn't expect this. Noel Jaylen Carter is the only man I have been with like that, and for him to suggest that I just casually sleep around is appalling."

Trying to sound reasonable, Danetta said, "If I was in his shoes, and had just been told that I have a daughter after no communication with the mother for seven years, I'd ask for a DNA test, because you just never know."

"Well, I know. And he is out of his mind if he thinks that I'm going to consent to having my daughter's mouth swabbed just so he can be convinced of something that should be obvious."

"I'm trying not to roll my eyes at you Ryla."

This conversation was confusing Ryla. Danetta was supposed to be on her side. "Huh? Why do you want to roll your eyes at me and not at Noel? He's the one being unreasonable."

"Ryla, you kept his child from him for seven years."

Now Ryla rolled her eyes. "Why does everybody keep harping on that?" Ryla understood that what she had done to Noel was wrong and a very big deal. But her snarky defense mechanism kept showing up, even when she knew there was no place for being snarky in this conversation.

"Okay, so, I can tell that you're not going to listen to a word I have to say because you're already getting defensive," Danetta said, and then added, "But if anything is going to get through to you tonight, let it be this. . . . You owe that man an apology, and you need to do whatever you have to in order to make things right so that Jaylen can have both her mother and father in her life from this point on."

Ryla took in a deep breath and then slowly exhaled. "I hear you. And I'm sorry about trying to be funny at a time like this. I know this isn't an easy situation for any of us."

"Ryla, girl, what are you going to do?"

Danetta sounded concerned, and Ryla appreciated that. "I guess I'm going to go along to get along, like you suggested. But if he tries to bring lawyers into this so he can steal my kid away from me, I'm going to need help finding an attorney. Do you know of anyone that might be able to help me?"

"If I don't, I'm sure Marshall does. Hopefully, it won't come to that, but if it does you know that we've got your back."

"Thanks, girl. I hope I don't have to call

in this favor, but it's good to know that I can get an attorney if I need to." Ryla was a bit calmer by the time she and Danetta hung up.

Jaylen was spending the night at her mom's, so she didn't have to leave the house again tonight. Exhausted, Ryla threw her pajamas on without even thinking about showering first. She jumped in the bed, and before fear could overtake her mind about Noel meeting his daughter for the first time, she imagined the smile that would surely be on Jaylen's face tomorrow and then calmly drifted off to sleep.

CHAPTER 3

"I need a drink," Noel told his brother, Donald, as they sat in his library. Donald pastored a church in Houston, and whenever Noel was in the city he bunked with him.

Donald leaned back in his chair and studied his younger brother. When he spoke, his words were measured. "How does a man of purpose sabotage his own future?"

Noel shook a finger at him. "Not now, Donald. Please save the philosophy for a man who hasn't just been told that he has a seven-year-old daughter that he knows nothing about."

Shaking his head, Donald said, "I remember meeting Ryla when the two of you were an item in college. She seemed like a very nice young lady."

"Yeah, well, looks can be deceiving. But I guess I was just too blinded by her beauty to notice the deception that lurked be-

31

neath." Noel pulled himself out of his seat and stood in front of the window, looking out at the other houses that surrounded his brother's spacious home. Just as his brother's home was filled with a wife and three kids, Noel imagined that children ran the halls of most of the rest of the suburban homes out here also.

And for the first time in his adult life, Noel realized that although his house was larger than many in this suburb, his brother and the neighbors around him had homes with families residing within. Every time Noel entered his own house, the echo of emptiness welcomed him.

He turned back to his brother, weariness showing in his eyes. "What am I going to do, Donald? How can I go back there tomorrow and meet a child that I'm not really sure belongs to me?"

"But I thought you told me that you and Ryla were in a monogamous relationship?"

Noel jabbed a finger at his chest. "I was monogamous. . . . I thought Ryla was, too. But we both know that I've been wrong before."

"What do you feel in your heart? Do you think Jaylen is yours?"

Noel's eyes closed with the weight of what he was going through. "I still can't believe that Ryla gave Jaylen my middle name but never said a word to me about this baby." He shook his head as he flopped back into his chair. He thought about the years he spent drinking, gambling and womanizing. He'd ruined his reputation so badly that he'd almost lost his way. "Things in my life could have been so different if I had known that I had a child."

"I realize that this is difficult for you. It would be difficult for any man to discover that the woman he loved and practically idealized has done something like this to him. But, my brother, you've got to keep the faith."

Noel knew that his brother spoke the truth and everything he said was for his own good. Several years ago, Donald had found him passed out in a bar where the patrons had not only taken pictures of his inebriated state, but had posted them online. By the next morning, CNN, MSNBC and every other news station had documented his fall from grace. They focused the world's attention on the fact that the great Noel Carter's knee injury had occurred during negotiations for his second three-year deal. The first contract had earned him five million a year, and this contract was about to double that, but then the knee injury happened, rendering the contract null and void. The newscasters had speculated that the voided contract had sent Noel on a drinking binge.

Only Noel and Donald knew that Noel's wounds went deeper than a voided contract. By the time that contract had been voided, Noel had already made enough money from his last basketball contract and endorsement deals to keep him living in luxury for a very long time. And Noel had business interests that would earn him more money in years to come. So, the loss of a simple contract didn't bother him much. Not being able to play the game he loved, and not having the woman he loved by his side was what had bothered him the most.

Since his basketball days, he'd invested in the stock market and a few urban renewal projects. Some stocks lost money, but the majority of his investments were making money. His urban renewal projects provided him with a community focus and reminded Noel of his desire to do more for his people. So, he'd put his hat in the race for the House of Representatives. They were acting like clowns right now with John Boehner as their leader, but Noel was still convinced that he could get in there and do some good. His campaign manager had warned him that the race would be an uphill battle because of all the drinking and womanizing he'd done in the past, but Noel had assured Ian that he was on solid ground. Now Noel wondered how many votes Ian would predict that he'd lose because of an illegitimate child.

"Do you want to pray, Noel?" Donald finally asked.

"I'm not sure what I want right now, Donald. I just know that I'm starting to feel that same hurt that drove me to the bottle in the first place."

"Mommy, Mommy, do I smell French toast?" Jaylen asked as she ran into the kitchen with her grandmother trailing behind.

Jaylen's favorite breakfast was French toast, and considering the news that Ryla had to deliver this morning, she figured that she'd better step her game up from the Cap'n Crunch, cereal she let Jaylen eat on Saturday morning. "And check it out," Ryla boasted. "I got you some strawberry syrup, powdered sugar and whipped cream."

Jaylen jumped for joy. "Just like we put on the waffles. Is this a special day or something?"

Okay, maybe she went a bit overboard,

but it wasn't every day that a little girl met her father for the first time. Noel had been so angry last night that he hadn't told her what time he would be back today. But she wasn't concerned about that, because if she knew nothing else, she knew that Noel Carter would be ringing her doorbell at his earliest convenience today. "It's not a special day, honey. But let's hurry up and eat, because there is something I'd like to talk to you about." Ryla turned and looked at her mom with imploring eyes. "Do you think you can hang out with us for a little while this morning?"

Juanita Evans-Berkley gave her daughter a big Texas smile as she sat her Coach purse down on the counter. "Are you kidding? For French toast with strawberry syrup, I'll hang out with y'all all day."

"Thanks, Mom," Ryla said, grateful that she would have a shoulder to lean on today. "Well, ladies, help me set the table so we can eat."

Ryla went to the refrigerator and took out the apple juice and orange juice, while Juanita took the plates out of the cabinet. Jaylen grabbed the napkins and forks. As Ryla put three glasses on the table her hand was shaking a bit.

Juanita glanced at Ryla. "Is everything okay?"

Ryla poured apple juice for Jaylen and then picked up the orange juice to pour herself and her mother a glass. "Sure, everything's okay," she said. But then the doorbell rang and Ryla almost dropped the juice. She gripped the orange juice bottle with a firmer hand and poured the juice in the glasses. She then put both juices back in the refrigerator and started chewing on her index finger.

"What's wrong?" her mother asked.

"Nothing's wrong," Ryla hurriedly said. "Why do you think something's wrong?"

"Well, for one thing, you're chewing on your finger. You only do that when you're trying to figure out how to get out of something. The doorbell has rung twice so far, but you haven't yet moved an inch to answer it."

Ryla took her finger out of her mouth and stepped away from the stove. "Can you fix Jaylen's plate while I go and see who's at the door?"

"Sure thing, hon," her mother said with a lifted brow.

Ryla took baby steps all the way to the front door. She fully expected Noel to show up again today, but not at ten in the morning. She had hoped he would at least give her until noon to break the news to their daughter. But as she looked out the peep-hole at the double-fudge fine black man standing on her porch, her suspicions were confirmed. She had to take a moment to study his face before opening the door. From his short fade to the well-manicured goatee, to his Hershey's Kiss chocolate skin, everything on Noel was perfection.

Well, everything but the scowl on his face as he pushed the buzzer several times in a row. Ryla swung the door open. "My good-ness, do you really need to wake the neigh-borhood?"

"I've been standing here for five minutes. And I know it doesn't take that long to get to the front door in your house."

Was that supposed to be some sort of crack about the size of her house? She put her hand on her hip and protested, "I was busy. And you did come over here without calling first."

"Do I have your number?" Noel rhetori-cally asked.

Noel's voice was rising, so Ryla stepped out on the porch and closed the door behind her. "You might want to keep it down a bit."

With nostrils flaring, Noel said, "I didn't

come over here to play games with you, Ryla. Is Jaylen home this morning or not?"

Nodding, she said, "She and my mother just arrived. But I haven't had time to tell her about you yet."

"When do you suppose you'll get around to that?" he asked, in a sarcasm-infused tone.

"She's eating breakfast right now. I was going to tell her as soon as she finished." She tried to shoo him off the porch. "So, can you just come back in about an hour or two?"

Noel's feet were firmly planted. "I'm not leaving until I meet Jaylen, so I hope you've fixed enough breakfast for me."

"Why do you have to be such a bully? Can't you understand that I need to break this to Jaylen gently?" Ryla knew that denying Jaylen the access to her father was wrong, even though her reason for doing so was to save her daughter from heartache later down the line. Ryla needed to clean up her own mess. She needed to make sure she didn't do any further harm to her daughter.

"I thought you said that she's been asking to meet me for a year now." He looked at her as if they were having a "duh" moment. "The simplest thing to do would be for both of us to go in there, sit down with Jaylen and tell her how you kept her from me all these years."

Ryla's mouth fell open. "You wouldn't dare do something like that."

"You don't think so . . . ? Watch me." Noel stepped away from Ryla and put his hand on the doorknob.

Ryla grabbed his arm. "Okay, okay, you win."

He turned back around. "And what exactly have I won, Ryla?"

"You don't have to leave. I'll go inside and talk to Jaylen right now, just go back to your car for a minute."

With a raised eyebrow he asked, "How long?"

"Give me ten minutes." As he got ready to step off the porch, Ryla grabbed his arm again. "You won't say anything bad about me to Jaylen, will you?"

"That depends," Noel said with a devilish grin. "Have you been saying anything bad about me in all these years that you've had her to yourself?"

Shaking her head at the notion, Ryla said, "That's ridiculous, Noel. I've never said a bad word about you to Jaylen!"

"Oh, you haven't said anything bad about me to Jaylen, so just who have you been running me down to?"

Before Ryla could think of a way to avoid telling Noel that she had indeed been talking about him to her two closest friends, Danetta and Surry, the front door opened. Ryla swung around and, as if in slow motion, she watched Jaylen look up at Noel and make the connection.

Ryla panicked. "Go back in the house for a minute, Jaylen. Mommy is talking to someone right now," Ryla said breathlessly.

But Jaylen swung open the screen door and jumped into Noel's arms and kissed his face. "Daddy! I'm so glad you came. I've been waiting my whole life to meet you." She kissed him again as she said, "Now I know why Mommy fixed my favorite breakfast. This is a special day."

CHAPTER 4

Noel had experienced a lot of things in his thirty years on earth. He'd been a superstar on the basketball court since grade school, graduated college with honors, was a first-round draft pick, had earned a championship ring his second year in the NBA and had become a millionaire several times over. But he'd never experienced anything like the joy he was now feeling as Jaylen hugged and kissed him. He gave her a tight never-want-to-let-you-go kind of hug. And then Noel put her down and stepped back. He had to be mindful that the DNA test had yet to be done, and as far as he knew, Jaylen could belong to another man. It could've been Ryla's sick, twisted mind that decided it would be a good thing to give another man's child his middle name. Not knowing what else to do, Noel stuck his hand out and said, "Hi, I'm Noel Carter."

Jaylen giggled as she shook her father's

hand. "Silly. I know who you are."

That's right, Noel reminded himself, Ryla did tell him that Jaylen kept an old photo of him and Ryla on her nightstand. "I wasn't sure that you would recognize me from an old photo. I have aged a bit since then," Noel said in a deeper, older man's tone.

Jaylen laughed again as she told him, "I saw you on the TV, too. You look the same."

Noel turned to Ryla for clarification on this. Had Jaylen been watching one of his old basketball games? Had Ryla taped his games and watched them as a way of having him around her . . . why hadn't she just picked up the phone and called him?

"Jaylen and my mom went to Dallas for the weekend and she saw one of your ads for Congress. Congratulations, by the way. I guess you finally found a way to help your community." Ryla was biting her finger again.

"Yeah, I'm finally pulling it all together," he told her as he racked his brain, trying to remember when he'd shared this particular dream with Ryla.

The front door opened again, and with that same big Texas grin, Juanita Evans said, "Well, hello, Noel. It's about time you showed up around here." She opened the door wide. "Y'all might as well get off the porch and come on in the house. We can all sit down and catch up over breakfast."

Jaylen grabbed Noel's hand and began pulling him toward the door. "Come on, Daddy, we've got the bestest breakfast ever this morning."

"French toast," Juanita said.

Noel rubbed his stomach. "It's one of my favorite breakfast meals also. So, I'll gladly join you."

Jaylen stopped walking and looked up at Noel in awe. "We have a favorite thing together?"

Noel smiled. Jaylen was speaking in seven-year-old language, but he knew exactly what she meant. "Yes, little one, you and I like the same kind of breakfast."

Noel followed Juanita and Jaylen in the house, and the smile left his face as he glanced back at Ryla. The look he gave her simply said, you've got some explaining to do.

Sitting at the breakfast table stuffing her face with more starch than she had put in her body in over a week, Ryla noticed that she was not receiving the you've-got-some-explaining-to-do looks from just Noel, but from her mother also. The beautiful and sophisticated Juanita had never fathomed that a woman would walk away from a man who could provide for her in ways she couldn't provide for herself. But Ryla was looking for more than a checkbook kind of man. She wanted love, respect and faithfulness. Noel had proven himself to be unfaithful, so Ryla had had no choice but to leave him or end up like her mother.

After breakfast, Jaylen turned to Noel and said, "Wanna see my room?"

Noel Stood. "Sure thing. Lead the way."

Jaylen stepped back as she looked up at her father. "Whoa. You know, you're a lot taller than I expected. I hope I'm not going to be so tall."

"I don't think you have anything to worry about. My mom and my sister are both about five-seven."

"Good," was all Jaylen said before turning to march off to her room. Noel followed close behind, smiling but also appearing to be suppressing a giggle.

When they were alone in the kitchen, Juanita turned to Ryla and said in an accusatory manner, "Well, he certainly doesn't look like a man who wants nothing to do with his child."

Ryla picked up the plates off the table and took them over to the sink.

"Don't try to ignore me, Ryla Evans,

because I can tell you right now that I am fighting mad."

Ryla turned around and leaned against the sink. She had asked her mother to stay for breakfast because she wanted to tell her and Jaylen about Noel coming for a visit, and then she had intended to explain the lie she'd told her mother when she'd come home pregnant with no husband. "I know I owe you an explanation."

Juanita's hands went to her hips in outrage. "I want to know what you did and I want to know it right now."

"Okay, Mom, calm down."

Running a hand through her honey-blond bob, Juanita said, "I'm confused, Ryla. I really don't understand what is going on, so please enlighten me."

Ryla lifted a hand, trying to bring her mother's volume down a notch. "I know I told you that Noel wanted nothing to do with Jaylen . . . but the truth is that I — I never told him that I was pregnant."

Juanita shook her head in disbelief. "Ryla, now, why would you do something like that to Jaylen?"

"I wasn't trying to do anything to Jaylen but protect her from heartache," Ryla said, trying to defend her actions.

"What are you talking about? How could

not allowing your child to have a relationship with her father protect her from heartache?" Juanita's voice was just above a whisper now.

"Well, for one thing, she wouldn't have to go through what I went through."

"Your father was with you throughout your adolescent years, Ryla. You were a daddy's girl and loved every minute of it."

Ryla sat back down at the kitchen table. "Yeah, but when he left you, he left me, too. He started a whole new family and just forgot all about me." She looked her mom square in the face as she declared, "I've never gotten over how he treated me. And I could never put Jaylen through that."

Juanita walked over to her daughter, putting an arm around her, and said, "Not every man is like your father, sweetheart. Jaylen has missed the opportunity of having a father in her life for all these years, so please don't stand in their way any longer. You fear things that may never happen."

But Ryla knew that her fears were founded by facts. Because she'd already seen how unfaithful Noel could be with her own eyes, and she didn't know if she could ever get over that. "Okay, Mom, I'll try."

However, before she could fix her mind around working out a solution so that Noel could be just as much a part of Jaylen's life as she was, he came back into the kitchen and asked to speak with her in private. Ryla got up from her seat and followed Noel outside to his Escalade.

Once they were by the side of the truck, Noel turned to her and said with pride in his voice, "She's a pretty amazing kid."

Thinking this was their time to share, Ryla perked up and said, "And she's smart, too, Noel. Her teachers are constantly telling me how quickly she learns and moves on to the next subject with ease and understanding."

"My mother used to tell me that the teachers said I was so smart that they couldn't keep up with me when I was in elementary school." Then his eyes clouded over with sadness as he said, "I've missed a lot of her life."

"I know," Ryla admitted. And then as if she had thought of something that would help him look on the bright side, she said, "But, Noel, you were running around living the single life and doing all sorts of crazy things the first five years of Jaylen's life — you wouldn't have had time for her anyway."

Anger replaced sadness as he ripped into her. "Don't tell me what I didn't have time for. You never gave me the chance. And maybe I wouldn't have gotten myself in so much trouble if I had known that I had a daughter to take care of. Did you ever think about that?"

"I know you're not trying to blame me for all the womanizing and drinking you did while in the NBA?"

"I see that you know how to read the tabloids. It's a shame that you couldn't figure out how to pick up a phone and use it."

"I didn't have your number," she protested.

"You had my mom's home number, and you knew her address. So, you have no excuse for what you did — you're just selfish." He shook his head. "I had no idea that you could be so heartless."

"Heartless!" she exploded. "That's rich, coming from a cheat."

His eyebrows furrowed as he questioned her. "What are you talking about? I never needed to cheat. . . . I won or lost all of my games fair and square."

"I'm not talking about basketball," Ryla said with a roll of her eyes. "Everything doesn't start and end with a basketball."

"Then what are you talking about?"

Ryla hugged her arms around her chest and changed the subject. "I'm not going to even go there with you. All we need to talk

49

about is Jaylen and that's it."

"Whatever." Noel was frustrated and knew he needed to get out of there before he said some things he'd end up regretting. "So, when can we schedule the DNA test?"

Ryla uncrossed her arms as she swung around to face off with Noel. "You just met Jaylen. Can you honestly tell me that you don't see the resemblance between the two of you?"

He nodded. "She has my complexion, my nose and my eyes, but the rest is all you." He waved a hand in the air as he said, "Don't get me wrong. After spending time with Jaylen, I do believe that she's mine, but you've already wronged me once on this. So, I'm going to make sure that I'm not being put in a trick bag by you." He then repeated for emphasis, "So, what date is convenient for you to do the DNA test?"

CHAPTER 5

Two Weeks Later

"Are you happy now?" Ryla asked Noel as they held the results of the DNA test in their hands. Noel was indeed the father and although it took two weeks to confirm that fact, Noel had traveled to Houston both weekends and spent time with Jaylen.

"Actually, no, I'm not happy," Noel responded.

Ryla's jaw hung low, as she thought Noel was saying that he wasn't happy to be Jaylen's father.

He continued, "I've only been able to spend a couple of weekends with my seven-year-old daughter and now I have a campaign to focus on, so I can't keep coming to Houston on the weekends."

Since he wasn't all that polite to her when he came for his weekend visits, Ryla really couldn't say that she'd miss him that much. But still she said, "That's too bad, Noel.

51

But I'm sure Jaylen will understand as long as you let her know what's going on."

The smirk on Noel's face couldn't be disguised as he said, "Actually, it's too bad for you. Because since today is Jaylen's last day of school and she is now officially on summer break, I intend to spend as many days as possible with my daughter this summer."

"What are you saying, Noel? You just told me that you'll need to be in Dallas, so I don't see how you'll be able to spend the summer with Jaylen."

He held up his paternity test, so Ryla could get a real good look at the 99.99999 percentage points that proclaimed him as Jaylen's father. "This little paper, and the fact that you kept my child from me for years, ensures that Jaylen will be able to spend the summer with me."

From his comment, Ryla figured that Noel was thinking about taking her to court, so she said, "I thought we agreed to leave lawyers out of this?"

"Woman, you must think I'm a fool," he said as he towered over her. "Why shouldn't I get my lawyer involved when I'm dealing with someone like you?"

Ryla started chewing her fingers as she tried to come up with something that would get Noel to see reason. He had accused her of trying to put him in a trick bag, but now she realized that he had put her in one. Noel had wanted that DNA test so he'd have proof that he was Jaylen's father. Then no one could deny him his rights, and she had fallen in line and gave him all the ammunition he needed to fight her in court. "Noel, can you just tell me what you want? Maybe we can work this out without involving outside parties."

"You just know that you're in the wrong. That's why you don't want to involve anyone else."

She held up a hand, trying to halt his incoming tirade. "I understand why you would see it that way."

"Ha." He laughed. "Me and the entire world would be able to see how wrong you are."

"Okay," she said calmly. She didn't want to argue with Noel. She wanted to try to work with him, so he could get out of his angry, win-at-all-cost mode. Ryla knew that an angry Noel was also a determined Noel. And when Noel set his mind to something, he would be dead set on finishing it. "I understand that you're upset, Noel. But can you please tell me what you want so we can work something out?"

"I want Jaylen in Dallas with me for the summer."

She got in negotiation mode. "Why don't we start with a weekend or even a week? I could bring her up and then you could bring her back to me. Or I could even come back and get her if your schedule is too busy."

"No."

She backed up, stared at him for a moment. "What do you mean, no? I'm trying to work with you. So, you need to work with me also."

"No," he said again. "You've had Jaylen for seven years, and I want her for the entire summer. That's the beginning and end of my negotiation."

When she didn't readily respond, he said, "What's your answer?"

"Dang, even your opponents on the court were able to at least dribble before they took a shot. Just hold on, I'm thinking."

Noel took out his cell phone.

"Who are you calling?" Ryla asked as he unlocked his phone and searched through his contacts.

"I'm looking for my attorney's number. If you and I can't settle this, then I'm going to pursue other options."

"Okay, okay," Ryla said. "She can come

with you for the summer. I just have one stipulation."

"And that is?" Noel asked while putting his phone away.

"I have to come with her."

"Oh, heck no. I am not about to spend my summer with you," Noel raged.

"I could think of better things to do than spend my summer with a grouch, too. For one thing, I have a new business to get off the ground. But we need to think about Jaylen, Noel. She needs her mother. And you're going to be busy with the campaign, so you won't be able to watch out for her all the time. You'll need me there, as well."

Relenting, because he knew she was right, Noel said, "Okay, you can come, but I have a stipulation myself."

"What's that?"

"Stay out of the way."

With that, Noel entered his SUV and backed out of the driveway, leaving her with no doubt that fun had just been canceled for the summer. Noel wanted nothing to do with her. Even though she had been the one to leave, Ryla had not been able to purge Noel from her heart and mind. She was still in love with the man. Ryla ached every time she saw him. She only wished she could go back in time and change what had happened. . . . She would have stayed and fought for their love. But to accomplish that she would actually have to send that time machine back in time to when her father divorced her mother for his twenty-one-year-old girlfriend. Or go back to when her mother's new boyfriend tried to make a move on her, or when her mother went through divorce number two, because, big surprise, the mongrel cheated on her.

After what she watched her mom go through, Ryla swore she would never let a man cheat on her. Every one of her friends had warned her about dating Noel. They said that a big-time alpha dog like Noel Carter would never be anything but a player. But Ryla didn't want to believe them. Noel loved her and she loved him. Then she caught him kissing Cathy O'Dell after the play-off game. That happened to be the same day that Ryla had planned to tell Noel about the baby. But then she had visions of Noel walking out on her and her baby, refusing to have anything to do with his own child, just as her father had done. She then dropped out of college and ran from Noel and every man who would surely be another heartache. But now Noel was back, and her heart was aching for him in ways it hadn't in seven long years.

Ryla went into the garage to grab her and Jaylen's suitcases. She would need to start packing.

After bringing their luggage into the house, she sat down on her sofa and called her mother. Every bit of Ryla's event-planning skills had been garnered from Juanita Evans-Berkley. The woman had style and grace and decorating skills that were second to none. Her mother had also just taken an early retirement from the publicity coordinator position she'd held with the government for twenty years. Juanita had big plans of traveling around the world and finding husband number three, but Ryla needed to put those plans on hold for a little while. "Hey, Mama," she said when Juanita picked up the phone.

"Hey, yourself. What are you and my wonderful granddaughter doing today?"

Ryla sighed. "It looks like we're going to be packing."

"Oh, really, where are you going?"

"Noel now has the DNA evidence to prove that he's Jaylen's father, and he has informed me that he simply can't live without his daughter being in Dallas with him this summer."

"Oh, I'm so thankful that he wants to

spend time with Jaylen," Juanita excitedly said.

Ryla knew her mother was thinking about how Ryla's own father basically discarded her when he began his new life with his teenage bride. And at that moment, she had to admit that it felt good to know that Noel wanted to include his child in his life no matter how busy he was. "I'm glad you're happy about this, Mom, because I'm going to need your help."

"Tell me what you need. I'm all ears."

Ryla hesitated for a moment, but just a moment. She needed to be in Dallas with her child, so she needed help from her mom. "I know you wanted to travel this summer, but I was hoping that you would stay around for a little while and help me with my new business so I can go to Dallas with Jaylen."

Juanita was silent.

"Come on, Mom, I need your help." Ryla was prepared to go to her mother's house and get down on her hands and knees and beg if she had to.

"Well, I did have plans for this summer," Juanita began.

Ryla rolled her eyes, but held her tongue.

"But I don't want you to be without Jaylen for the summer, so I can help you out for a month or two."

"Thanks, Mom, I really appreciate this."

As she hung up with her mother, Ryla felt better about the situation. She would get everything in order and be prepared when Noel came back for Jaylen. The last thing Ryla wanted was for Noel to think she was jerking him around again. Ryla knew that judges frowned on parents who tried to keep the children away from the other parent. If she pushed Noel, he could end up with sole custody of Jaylen, with her begging for visitation. And that just couldn't happen.

Although Noel thought he came up with the perfect solution for spending time with his daughter, the idea wasn't going over so well at his campaign headquarters.

"Are you insane?" Ian Walters, Noel's longtime friend and campaign manager, asked after Noel told him what was going on.

"Why does the fact that I want to be with my daughter while I'm campaigning sound like such a bad idea?" Noel demanded as he sat behind his desk with his leg propped on the table.

"Do you realize how much bad press I have already had to deflect from this campaign?"

"Yeah, yeah, yeah." Noel waved away the problem. "I've heard it all before. The bad boy turned politician is the way they like to paint me. But I'm not just some former bad boy. I care about this community and I want to make a difference. I'm not doing this for fame or fortune — I clearly already have both of those."

With a frustrated sigh, Ian tried again. "I know that your reasons for running for office are honorable. But Dan Bridges believes that he is honorable also, and he thinks he has just as much right to claim that empty seat as you do. Dan Bridges is a family man with no skeletons in his closet that I've been able to find. But you have just pulled out a closet full, and now you want to bring her on the campaign trail." He lifted his hands in surrender. "I'm telling you, my friend, this is suicide."

Noel took his feet down from the top of his desk. Then he stretched and leaned back in his chair as he studied Ian a moment. They had been friends since high school, so Noel was willing to give him a pass this one time. But he wasn't about to let anyone speak negatively about his daughter. She was a part of him; he'd been denied access to her for too long as it was. He had no plans of waiting until the campaign was over to build a relationship with the most important girl in the world to him. "I'm going to say this once and once only, Ian. I will not be denied my daughter. I would rather lose this election than spend another day without her. Is that understood?"

Ian threw up his hands again. "You're the boss," he said as he walked out of the office, shaking his head and mumbling something about the press and a field day.

CHAPTER 6

The first time Ryla walked into Noel's campaign office in Dallas, Texas, she wanted to turn around and walk right back out. But Jaylen was pulling her toward her father's office with a great big grin on her face. "Daddy, Daddy, Daddy," Jaylen called out as she ran toward Noel.

As the people in the campaign office turned and gawked at the little girl screaming for her daddy, Noel picked her up and hugged her to him. "Hey, baby girl. I'm so glad that you're finally here. I was missing you."

"Mmph," Ryla said.

Noel put Jaylen down and turned to Ryla. "How was the drive up?"

"Fine," she answered too quickly.

"Did you have a hard time finding the place?" Noel asked.

Ryla began to look around the small office so she wouldn't have to look Noel in the face, and then said, "I do have a GPS, you know."

Noel turned to his campaign manager. "Ian, do you mind sitting out here with Jaylen? I need to speak with Ryla for a moment."

Ian turned to Jaylen and asked, "Would you like me to show you around the office, so you can see what your Daddy does all day?"

"I sure would." Jaylen grabbed Ian's hand and skipped down the hall beside him.

Noel walked into his private office and held the door open until Ryla stepped in. The moment he closed the door, he swung around and faced off with her. "Thank you for bringing my daughter to me. Now please feel free to leave at any moment."

Ryla harrumphed and folded her arms. "I wish I would leave my daughter to you and Cathy O'Dell."

With a lifted eyebrow he asked, "What does Cathy have to do with anything?"

Oh, now he's going to play dumb, Ryla thought. But she had his *Cheaters for Dummies* handbook in the palm of her hand and was seconds away from hitting him upside the head with it. "I know what you and Cathy had going on when we were in college."

Noel stepped back, the look of confusion apparent on his face. "What are you talking about? Cathy and I never had anything *going on,* as you put it."

Waving his comment away, she got in his face. "Stop lying, Noel. Because I saw you and Cathy kissing after the play-off game."

His eyes took on a faraway look for a moment and when he turned back to Ryla, he said, "You left college right after the play-offs."

She stepped away from him and walked over to the big window in his office and looked out at the staff through wooden venetian blinds. Ryla starred straight at Cathy O'Dell, wondering why she alone hadn't been enough for Noel. Why he had to go and ruin everything they had by cheating on her. If he had spit in her face, it would have hurt her less than how she ended up feeling after walking into that locker room and seeing Noel with another woman.

From the day Ryla's father walked out so he could start a new family, she swore that she'd never marry a man like her father. The day she discovered that she was pregnant was supposed to be a happy day. Not wanting to throw Noel's concentration off, she decided to wait until after the big play-off game to tell him about the baby. Ryla had been so excited that his team had won. And as she walked into the locker room to tell him her news, she just knew that he would feel as if he had won twice that night.

"Was Cathy the reason you left without as much as a goodbye to me?"

She heard the anger in his voice. But as far as she was concerned, all her sympathy for him went out the door the moment she saw Cathy behind that desk, taking calls and barking out orders as if she was working hard to help her man see all his dreams come true. Ryla should have been the one standing by his side, helping him get to the finish line, as the first lady did for the president. With a bit of her own anger, she turned to him. "You were the reason I left."

He stood there, visibly trying to rein in his fury. "I don't know how I could have been the reason you left. You never even gave me a chance."

"You squandered the chance I gave you —" Ryla pointed out toward the office staff "— with Ms. Phone Girl out there."

"Go home, Ryla. Jaylen and I don't need you here."

"Have you lost your mind?" She stepped to him again. "I am not about to leave my daughter here so you can flaunt your women in her face."

Noel laughed.

"I'm not playing with you, Noel Carter." She was shaking a finger in his face. "You are not going to parade your women around my daughter. I won't allow that."

"Whoa," he said, lifting his hands. "You're being a bit overdramatic, don't you think?"

As Ryla realized that she was acting like someone off her meds, she dialed it back a bit. "All I'm asking is that you keep Cathy away from Jaylen."

"That's going to be a little difficult, since we have a small office of about fifteen people and everyone is running on top of each other as it is."

"Well, aren't there other campaigns that she can go work for?"

He stared at her for a moment. "Are you serious?"

Ryla knew she was being unreasonable, but she just couldn't back down. She felt violated by Cathy just as she would have felt violated by any thief that kicked in her front door and stole something from her. She put her hands on her hips and declared, "Either she goes or I'm taking Jaylen back home."

"Then I call my lawyer," Noel volleyed back as he walked over to his desk and picked up the telephone.

"You said you wouldn't do that," Ryla protested, wondering if she had overplayed her hand.

"That was before you came to my campaign office and started making unreasonable demands." He pushed a few buttons on the telephone.

Ryla pushed the disconnect button on the phone. "Don't do this Noel. We don't need to get lawyers involved."

Still holding the receiver, Noel's voice elevated. "If you think you're going to come in here and make demands after keeping my child from me for seven years, then I think we need a third party to straighten this out. Because I'm not letting you take another minute of my time with Jaylen away from me."

Ryla surrendered. "Okay, okay, you win. Jaylen Stays. . . . Just keep her away from your little girlfriend."

"She's not my girlfriend."

"Whatever." Ryla waved his comment off.

The door to Noel's office opened and Ian quickly stepped in and closed it behind him. "You might want to bring it down a few notches. And in case you were wondering, if they didn't figure it out when Jaylen ran through the office screaming, 'Daddy,

Daddy, Daddy,' you two have now informed the entire staff that Jaylen is your daughter." Ian was glaring at Noel as he leaned against the wall. "Oh." He held up a finger as if he needed to add one more thing. "They also know that Ryla kept her away from you for seven years."

"I don't see why this is an issue. I was going to tell them all anyway," Noel said.

Rising up from against the door, Ian walked toward Noel. "That is true. However, I just spent the last few minutes introducing Jaylen to everyone and not once did I mention that she was your daughter. Then, as Cathy was showing Jaylen how to work the phone system, everyone heard you yelling about Ryla keeping your daughter away from you for seven years."

Noel held up a hand. "Okay, I messed up. But we can trust our staff. They won't repeat anything I've said."

"We don't just have the staff out there this morning, Noel. We had a few vendors bringing in supplies. So, we'll be lucky if this information isn't reported by the nightly news."

"Noel, that's why you shouldn't have demanded that Jaylen accompany you this summer. You're only making trouble for your campaign that you don't need," Ryla said, trying to sound like the reasonable one in the room.

Noel turned on her. "Don't you go there with me. It wouldn't be necessary for me to get to know my daughter while I'm campaigning if you hadn't kept her from me all these years."

Tilting her head back, Ryla asked, "Do you really want to give the staff and the vendors things to talk about?" She suddenly turned to Ian and asked, "Where is my daughter?"

"She's fine. I left her with Cathy so that I could come in here and calm y'all down."

Ian was talking, but Ryla was walking. After hearing that her daughter had been left with man-stealing Cathy, she hadn't heard another word that Ian said. She swung the door open and rushed to Jaylen's side as if she needed a protector. "Come on, baby, let me take you to get some lunch."

"I can do that," Noel said as he approached the scene.

Cathy stuck out her hand to Ryla and said, "Hey, Ryla, I wasn't paying attention when you came in earlier. I had no idea that it was you. How've you been?"

Ryla quickly shook Cathy's hand and then let it go as if she would be in need of some disinfectant if she held on a second longer. "I've been good, and you?"

"I'm doing great now that I'm finally able to use my political science degree." Cathy put her hand on Noel's shoulder and said, "I just can't thank Noel enough for rescuing me from that boring accounting job I was in."

"I'm sure you've found many ways to thank him," Ryla said with a knowing look in her eyes. She then grabbed Jaylen's hand. "Come on, baby."

"Where are we going, Mommy?" Jaylen asked as Ryla tried to rush her out of Noel's campaign office.

"Yes, where are we going, Ryla?" Noel asked, keeping up with them.

Ryla swung around. "I'm sure you're busy, so you don't need to go to lunch with us. I'm sure I can find my way around."

Noel opened the door for them, and as Ryla and Jaylen walked outside, he said, "I'll tag along. I need to get Jaylen's suitcase out of your car anyway."

Ryla glared at Noel as they walked toward her car. "I wasn't trying to run off. I was going to bring her back."

"Well, this way I've got one less thing to worry about." As they reached her car, Noel said, "Pop your trunk."

"What for?" Ryla was beginning to get irritated by Noel constantly barking orders at her.

He gave her a "duh" look. "I need to get Jaylen's suitcase, remember?"

"Actually, you don't."

Noel turned to his daughter. "Jaylen, why don't you get in your mother's car, so she and I can decide where we're going for lunch."

"Okay, Daddy," Jaylen said as she joyously jumped into the backseat of the car.

Since it was hot out, Ryla got in the car, started it and turned on the air. She then got back out of the car and asked Noel, "What's the problem now?"

"What are you trying to pull?"

"I don't have the slightest idea what you're talking about." Indifference showed all over her face.

"You just said I don't need Jaylen's suitcase. So, are you telling me that you didn't bring her any clothes to wear when you knew that she was supposed to be staying with me for the summer?"

"I brought her clothes, Noel. But Jaylen won't be staying with you every night. My aunt lives in Dallas, so Jaylen and I will stay with her this summer and she can visit with you every day." She couldn't resist her last

71

dig, so she said, "That way, Jaylen won't interfere with your nightlife."

CHAPTER 7

Noel wasn't about to let Ryla run his show.
He had tried that in college and all he got
for his efforts was a broken heart. After getting himself through that ordeal, he'd sworn
that he would never let another woman take
a piece of his heart as they walked out of
his life. As a matter of fact, he now did the
walking.

Noel was in his office wearing his carpet
out as he tried to come up with a strategy
for dealing with Ryla. He adored Jaylen and
would forever be thankful that she was his
daughter. But when it came to dealing with
Ryla — that was another matter altogether.
The woman was driving him nuts with her
demands and drama. If she wasn't telling
him who Jaylen couldn't be around, she was
dictating how long he could keep her out at
night, even though Jaylen was on summer
break and didn't have anywhere in particular to be first thing in the morning.

Ryla was driving him to drink, or at least to think about drinking more than he had in years past. Noel prayed that he could stay away from alcohol and all the things that came with it. But to do that he would need to get Ryla off his back.

A knock on his door stopped Noel's pacing. "Come in," he said as he sat down on the leather couch in his office.

Ian stormed in, waving a newspaper around and looking as if somebody had stolen something from him. "I don't want to say I told you so. But for the record, I did tell you that bringing Jaylen on the campaign trail was a bad idea."

With his feet propped up on the coffee table, Noel let out a long-suffering sigh. "What's the problem now?"

Ian thrust the newspaper in Noel's face. "This means trouble for us, my friend."

Noel took the paper. The headline read, Former Bad Boy NBA Player Noel Carter Has a Baby Mama. Noel almost laughed at the headline. Because he knew the reason Gary Morrison had bothered to write the fit-for-a-tabloid piece was that he was a wannabe pro baller, trapped in a sportswriter's fat body. As he read further, he noted that the cruel reporter provided Jaylen and Ryla's full names, ages and the actual town in which they lived. He did everything but offer up their address and phone number.

Noel threw the newspaper against the wall as he stood and growled. "I want Gary fired for this one."

Shaking his head, Ian said, "Everything in that article is factual. You can't get the man fired for printing the facts."

"Come on, man. Everybody knows that Gary loves to trash me in his column simply because he got cut from the team the same year I got picked up. Now, if that doesn't show bias in reporting, I don't know what does."

"He can have as much bias as he wants, he just can't lie," Ian explained. He picked up the paper off the floor and added, "And anyway, there's worse news than this."

A storm cloud of hot anger brewed in Noel's eyes as he asked, "Did something happen to Jaylen as a result of this article?"

Ian waved the notion away. "No, nothing like that. It's just that this article has been out less than twenty-four hours and your poll numbers have already dropped."

Noel sat back down. "Polls fluctuate. We can't hang our hopes on one poll versus another. Last week you were cheesing because I was a point ahead of Dan Bridges."

"Noel, you have to understand. You are the underdog. Representative Samuel Dwight held that title for six consecutive terms before he died, and his party is not about to just lie down and give his seat to you."

"Yeah, but Bridges tried to align himself with the Tea Party, and the polls you love to talk about so much show that America is sick of tea. They'd rather have a job or at least an elected official who will actually do something to help the people."

Ian sat down across from Noel. "The odds are in your favor to win. But it will be an uphill battle, because many of the voters still remember you as a womanizing, gambling drunk, with more money to spend than sense. We need to convince them that you are a changed man. And I'll be honest with you, Noel. This article about you having a *baby mama* doesn't help us one bit."

"I don't know what you want me to do about it, Ian. I can't go back to the days when I didn't know I had a child, and even if I could, I don't want to."

"I'm not asking you to deny your child, Noel. I know that you can't do that."

Noel shrugged. "Well, then, I guess that's it. Lowlife reporters like Gary Morrison will try to make something of this, but I think people will understand that I didn't just run out and impregnate some random woman while handing out Vote for Noel Carter buttons. Jaylen is seven years old."

"I know that, and you know it, but if this news continues to circulate, we both know that you'll lose this election."

"What do you want me to do about it, Ian?"

"I'm glad you asked," Ian said with a sly grin. "Because I do have a solution."

"How painful will this solution of yours be?" Noel knew that Ian had his best interests at heart, but sometimes the man asked too much of him.

"That depends."

"On what?" Noel asked cautiously.

"On how you feel about marrying Ryla Evans."

"What? Have you lost your mind?" Noel prided himself on keeping a level head at stressful times. But Ian was raising his blood pressure with the nonsense he was talking. "Did you just ask me to marry the same woman who kept my child from me for seven years?"

"I know it's a lot to ask, but you really need to think this through. If you want to win this election, I think you need a wife in order to convince your constituents that as an elected official you won't be spending your time chasing women and missing important votes on the House floor as an elected official."

"I hear what you're saying, Ian. But I just can't trust Ryla. If she could do what she did to me and Jaylen, what else is she capable of?"

"Maybe she had a good reason for not telling you about Jaylen. Did you ever ask her why she left without telling you she was pregnant?"

"I don't have to. I figured out what happened about two seconds after she demanded that I fire Cathy."

"She did what?" Ian's eyes grew big with Noel's pronouncement.

"You heard me. And I think I know why," Noel said with a smirk on his face. As Ian listened intently, Noel continued, "Somehow she got it in her head that Cathy and I had something going on in college."

"Mommy, why don't you and Daddy live together?" Jaylen asked as Ryla was helping her out of the tub while drying her with a towel.

Ryla sighed, as she wrapped the towel around Jaylen and walked her down the hall to the guest bedroom her aunt allowed them to stay in. She didn't like having conversations with Jaylen about her father. Jaylen always ended up asking questions that were painful for Ryla to answer. "Your daddy and I aren't married, sweetheart, that's why we don't live together."

Jaylen lifted her arms and let her Princess Tiana gown slide down her body. "Why didn't you marry my daddy?"

"It's complicated, Jaylen. I really don't want to discuss this tonight."

As Jaylen climbed into bed and pulled the covers up, she said, "But you told me that you wanted to marry Daddy and that if you had the chance you would."

Ryla remembered their conversation well. Jaylen had been five and her best friend's mom had just remarried her children's father. Jaylen came running home with the news. Once she'd told Ryla everything about her friend's mom and daddy being so happy together again, she'd asked Ryla if she would remarry Noel. Ryla hadn't even bothered to correct Jaylen with the fact that she had never been married to Noel in the first place. Ryla had thought the entire conversation was moot because she never expected to see or hear from Noel again. So, she smiled and said, "If I ever got the chance, I would marry your dad in a heartbeat." Now those words were coming back to bite her.

Sitting at the edge of Jaylen's bed, Ryla tried her best to explain the situation. "Your dad and I are two different people now. He's changed and so have I."

"Yeah, but he's a really nice man and you're a really nice mom. You guys are perfect for each other. You just need to stop arguing over me so much and then you'll see what I see."

Everything was so easy when you were a seven-year-old who hadn't yet experienced heartbreak. "I wish it were that simple, baby, but sometimes life is more complicated than that."

Jaylen protested, "Daddy would marry you. Just stop arguing with him so much and you'll see."

Ryla laughed. "Okay, baby, I'll stop arguing with your daddy."

"And then you'll get married?" Jaylen persisted.

"If you say so, sweetheart." Ryla kissed Jaylen on the forehead, then stood and walked out of the bedroom, wondering how in the world she could explain the true facts to her daughter without crushing her spirit. Not to mention the fact that each day she spent with Noel brought back sweet memories of long ago when she loved him and he loved her. . . . Things were definitely getting more complicated.

CHAPTER 8

Noel was standing before a roomful of reporters asking one personal question after the next. Ever since he'd announced his candidacy for the House of Representatives, Noel had been trying to get some press. However, an ex-baller running for a House seat just wasn't sexy enough for the media. But now that he had some baby mama drama going on, the media was all over him.

"So when did you discover that you had a daughter?" called out one of the reporters.

"Is Jaylen happy to finally have her father in her life?"

Then the questions got more severe. "Did the mother think you would be a bad influence on her daughter? Is that why she didn't tell you about the child until now?"

"So does this mean you're back to your old love 'em and leave 'em ways? And can we expect any more children to pop up?"

Noel was swimming in a sea full of questions that he didn't want to answer. He braced his hands on the table in front of him as he contemplated walking out without answering any of their rude and insulting questions. "You know, I am running for the House of Representatives. Do you want to ask any questions about my plan to bring more good-paying jobs to our community? Or my thoughts on some of the issues that are at stake in this election?"

"We want to know if you plan on impregnating any more women without marrying them or providing support for the child?" another rude reporter yelled out.

Ian stood. "If anyone has questions concerning the House seat that Noel is running for, we'll be more than happy to respond, but this is getting a bit ridiculous."

Noel glanced toward the open doorway and noticed Ryla and Jaylen walking in. He wanted to bring this interrogation to an end right now so his daughter didn't have to hear any of the awful things being said. Then as he stood up preparing to leave the room, a reporter in the front said, "Three of your ex-girlfriends were interviewed this week. They confirmed that they don't have any illegitimate children by you, but considering your wild ways, they all think that more illegitimate children of yours will soon be popping up in need of DNA tests."

Noel's eyes were on Ryla. He saw the look of humiliation on her face, and at that moment he realized why she had fought so hard to keep both herself and Jaylen out of his world. Now he realized that she had probably been right about not bringing Jaylen on the campaign trail. But his need to have his daughter by his side overruled his common sense.

Noel stood and turned to the reporter, ready to blast him for daring to call his precious child illegitimate in his presence. Then suddenly Jaylen ran toward the stage, looking out at the sea of reporters, and took them on as if he had been giving her lessons on how to defend herself all her life.

"You can't call me names!" she shouted over the noise of the crowd. Then she said, "You can't call me that word, because I belong to my mommy and daddy and they are going to get married soon." For good measure, she added a *harrumph* on the end of her declaration.

Cameras began flashing as Jaylen hugged her father's side. Reporters moved closer to the table with gleams of "first scoop" in their eyes. "Can you confirm your daughter's statement, Noel?" a reporter in the first row asked.

"Is it true, Noel?" a reporter in the back of the room yelled out. "Are you turning in your player card for good?"

As the room erupted in laughter, Ryla ran onto the stage, quickly grabbed Jaylen and tried to make her way to escape. But suddenly three reporters descended upon her and Jaylen, blocking their path.

Like a hero, Noel came to their rescue and warned the reporters that his daughter was off-limits, looking around to ensure his message was clear. But before they could continue out of the room, one of the reporters shoved a microphone in Ryla's face and asked, "Can you confirm your daughter's statement? Are you and Noel going to be married soon?"

Ryla immediately turned to Jaylen, then back to the reporters. She opened her mouth, but before she could speak, Jaylen said, "Tell 'em, Mommy. Tell 'em how you can't wait to marry Daddy."

"Ma'am, is that true?" another reporter asked. "Are you excited to be marrying Noel Carter?"

"No comment," Ryla said, and then rushed out of the room, leaving Noel holding on to Jaylen's hand with a dumbfounded expression on his face.

The reporters then turned to Noel. "So,

when's the big day?"

He glanced at his little girl. She looked up at him, waiting and expecting him to be her knight in shining armor and save her from these mean old reporters who didn't believe her. He simply could not crush her spirit by denying the truth of her words. So, he picked Jaylen up and rushed out of the room without saying a word.

Back at the office, Noel was fuming as he sparred with Ian over the press conference. "I'm still trying to figure out why you even called this press conference today. You knew they wouldn't ask any serious questions in light of how a few of my ex-girlfriends blasted me on an entertainment news channel earlier this week."

"Those women are the reason we had to do this press conference today. Since they started flapping their gums about how you dated and dismissed them, your poll numbers have taken a dive."

"And meanwhile, one of them just earned herself a guest appearance on a popular reality show with scorned women who don't seem to be the least bit *real,*" Noel said, still fuming.

"Whether those women are real or not, you will soon have a *real* wife," Ian told him.

"Oh, no I won't." Noel wasn't about to get trapped by Ryla and her "no comment" crap. She could have just as easily said no and then rushed out of the room with Jaylen. Instead, she left his daughter behind for him to crush her dream. Noel knew how it felt to have dreams crushed, so there was no way he was going to do that to his kid, not in a million years.

"I don't see what the big deal is. You told me yourself that you were in love with Ryla during college, and the reason you dated so many women after college was because you hadn't met anyone who could take your heart back from her," Ian said.

"That was before I discovered just how heartless and cold-blooded she is."

Ian flopped down in his seat. "Look, Noel, I think it's time that you face the facts."

"And just what are these facts that you want me to face?" Noel sat down across from his campaign manager, snarling like an angry bull.

Ian sighed deeply as he said, "Your poll numbers have plummeted since your ex-girlfriends started sharing your bedroom secrets to anyone with a camera and a microphone."

"I can't stop them from talking, Ian. This is still a free country. And although I thought I treated every woman I dated with dignity, maybe they're right about the fact that I ended the relationship before giving them a chance."

"Yeah, but they didn't have to hire an attorney. I guess everybody wants their five minutes of fame," Ian said while shaking his head.

"Look, man, I can tell that this thing has got you worried. And if you're worried, then I should be, too. Just tell me what you think we can do to solve the problems my former lifestyle has created."

"I already told you what needs to be done, but you're not trying to hear me." Ian sounded as if he was tired of the conversation.

"So far it seems you've given me two bad choices. Marry Ryla or lose the election. There has to be some middle ground here."

Noel would take anything except the heartbreak that was sure to come if he married Ryla. When Ian didn't respond, Noel huffed, "Come on, Ian. There has to be another solution. I can't marry a woman I don't trust."

"If you marry another woman, it will look like you left your baby mama out in the cold yet again. Let's not forget that you haven't paid any child support in the past seven years."

"That's because I didn't know I had a child." Noel jerked out of his chair and stood by the window looking out at the street. He was as frustrated as a caged lion with no hope of escape. "Be honest with me, Ian. What are my chances of winning this race?"

"Without Ryla by your side, letting your constituents know that you're a changed man with your mind on government business rather than chasing skirts, I'd say the chances are slim."

Taking his lumps like a man, Noel said, "I'll go talk to Ryla."

CHAPTER 9

Ryla was a nervous wreck. After accepting Noel's invitation to dinner, she realized that she didn't have a thing to wear. She hadn't brought any after-five clothes with her on this trip. She'd brought a few sundresses with her from Houston, but somehow a sundress didn't seem appropriate for her first date with Noel in over seven years.

Ryla knew that Noel wasn't actually taking her on a date. This dinner would be used solely as an opportunity for them to discuss Jaylen. But Ryla allowed herself to dream for a moment. Being around Noel's campaign office for the past few weeks she and Jaylen had been in Dallas, Ryla began to realize that he didn't have anything going on with Cathy. They didn't look at each other like lovers, nor did they try to find reasons to be together. Matter of fact, when Cathy needed anything, she went directly to Ian. She rarely sought out Noel.

Ryla hadn't forgotten about the kiss the two of them shared while they were all in college. But since Noel appeared to be telling the truth about the current state of his relationship with man-stealing Cathy O'Dell, she had allowed herself to wonder what her and Jaylen's life would be like if she and Noel were back together.

It was with that in mind that Ryla went to the mall and found a slightly sexy, somewhat conservative cream-colored dress that stopped just above her knee. It clung to her just enough to emphasize her round butt. The dress actually made her appear to be a bit more curvaceous than she really was — sold.

As Ryla began walking out of the mall toward her car with her fabulous dress slung over her shoulder, a man approached her. Ryla became wary. The man wasn't dressed as if he had the kind of money her clients spent on the events she hosted, so she was almost positive that she hadn't met the man while working.

As he got closer, he said, "I'd like to show you something."

"That's okay, I'm kind of in a hurry," she said as she sidestepped him.

But the man then held up a small black book, and as Ryla read the words on it she became curious. The words on the front of the black book asked, "Who did Jesus die for?"

Ryla opened her mouth, wanting the man to either give her the answer or leave her alone. But before she could say anything, he opened the book. Instead of reading the answer to the question on the front of the little black book, Ryla saw two mirrors and then realized that she was staring at a reflection of herself. Ryla didn't get it. The world was full of people. So, why did that man show her a mirror that only had her reflection in it? Didn't Jesus die for all?

Ryla didn't have time to contemplate this, so she filed it away in her memory and decided to ask Danetta about it later. Her best friend, Danetta Windham, had recently joined her aunt's church and she knew more about spiritual matters than Ryla. And anyway, Ryla needed to concentrate on her hair, nails and outfit for her date later with Noel.

Okay, Noel hadn't actually called it a date. And maybe she shouldn't be so excited about going out to dinner with Noel Carter, her first and only love. But Ryla couldn't help it. Every minute she spent in the man's presence caused her to want more. She knew that he couldn't feel the same way about her because he was still angry about how she'd kept Jaylen away.

Every time she caught a glimpse of sorrow in Noel's eyes as he looked at Jaylen, she knew he was thinking about all the time he'd missed with his little girl. And Ryla was responsible for that. If only she could make him understand how fear of being with a man like her father had gripped her heart and mind and drained her of reason. As she'd watched Jaylen grow each year, Ryla had wanted so desperately to share those special moments with Noel. But every time she thought about locating him to tell him about his daughter, she would read about him dating another woman — never anything serious, just his flavor of the month.

A few of the women he'd dated had been movie stars. She'd loved going to the movies to see those actresses; that was, until they became Noel's new interest. She'd missed two Tyler Perry movies because actresses who had previously dated Noel had starring roles.

Ryla knew that her fears were no excuse for keeping a father away from his daughter, but every time she saw a picture of Noel with another woman, she thought of her father and his two marriages since he had left her mother. The first woman was practically a teenager, who quickly had three children then refused to allow Ryla to come to her house anymore. Her father, the Honorable Judge Stanley Evans, hadn't fought for her, either. Instead, he told Ryla that he would visit her and the two of them would have their own special time together. But that rarely happened, and by the time he'd divorced his teenage bride and moved on to wife number three, Ryla and her dad had stopped communicating altogether.

A slow tear trickled down her face as she thought of the pain her father had inflicted on her at such an early age. She'd fought hard to ensure that Jaylen never had to know the pain of waiting by the window, looking for a father who didn't keep his promises. But now that Noel was back around, Ryla's heart was softening toward him. She had wanted nothing more than to tell that reporter that, yes, she would marry Noel in a heartbeat.

If she thought it would make a difference, Ryla would beg Noel to forget about his anger and give their love another try. But Ryla wasn't so sure that her words would move Noel, so she'd simply said, "no comment," and walked out of the room. Ryla knew that although Noel would surely want to talk about Jaylen during their dinner tonight, he would also question her about not just saying no.

Part of the reason she didn't *just say no* had to do with Jaylen standing close by, looking up at her so hopefully. She didn't want to crush her daughter's dreams. The other reason was that she couldn't bear to crush her own dreams at that very moment, either. Saying no would have meant that she would have to stop dreaming about ever having a life with Noel Carter, and she had been dreaming that dream for almost a decade. Through the years she had hid her daughter from him, telling herself that she would willingly sacrifice her own heart so that Jaylen would never have to experience the heartbreak of watching her father walk out the door. But even through those times, Ryla couldn't stop herself from living out a lifetime of togetherness with Noel in her dreams.

As Ryla got in her car and drove to her aunt's house to get ready to meet Noel for dinner, she wiped away a few more tears. These tears, however, had nothing to do with her father — they were for heartbreak of a different kind.

Noel sat in a corner table at Stephan Pyles,

a restaurant that specialized in southwestern cuisine located in downtown Dallas. Noel enjoyed eating at this restaurant because chef Stephan Pyles's entrées were infused with smoky, spicy and aggressive flavors that so few restaurants were bold enough to try. The atmosphere was also cozy and intimate, which didn't hurt, since Noel would have to play things just right to get what he needed from Ryla.

As he sipped his wineglass full of sweet tea, minus all the Pimm's liqueur and Jeremiah Weed Sweet Tea vodka he used to liberally mix in, Noel looked over today's paper one last time. He shook his head as he laid the paper on the table. Ryla had been back in his life for less than a month and she was already causing him monstrous amounts of grief. Noel's focus should be one hundred percent on the election, but he could barely concentrate on that matter since his daughter and Ryla had come back into his life.

Noel didn't know if that was a good or bad thing. All he knew for sure was that he never wanted to experience the heartache of Ryla's abandonment eight years ago. He'd tracked her down at her mother's house and begged and pleaded with her to come back to him. But she had refused.

She'd never once mentioned Cathy, because if she had he would have told her that there was nothing to the kiss that Cathy gave him in the locker room.

When Cathy had attempted to kiss him, Noel had taken her arms from around his neck and politely explained that he was in love with Ryla and that their relationship meant everything to him. The night before, he and Ryla had lain in his bed discussing the type of wedding they wanted. Ryla had told him that she wanted to have their wedding and reception at the Four Seasons in Houston. And Noel wanted to do everything in his power to make her dreams come true. So, fooling around with Cathy wasn't an option. That was it, end of story.

Noel closed off the past as he glanced up and saw Ryla strutting toward his table. At that moment, Noel knew that Ryla didn't have an ounce of compassion for him. Because if she did, she would have never worn anything that accentuated her curves the way this particular dress did. The dress also showcased her beautiful legs. Noel checked his mouth for drool as he stood to welcome her to the table. "Thank you for joining me, Ryla."

"My pleasure. I've never dined at this restaurant before, so I was anxious to give it a try." She took a seat.

"Well, I hope you like it. I enjoy the smoky and spicy flavors of the cuisine." Noel sat back down and tried to avert his eyes, but he was having a hard time finding anything worth staring at besides the lovely woman seated across from him. Then his eyes stumbled across the newspaper he'd just glanced at moments ago. He picked it up and handed it to Ryla. "You've gotten me into a bit of a jam."

Ryla took the paper and read the headline, Big Day for Noel Carter. As she continued reading a bit of the story, she understood why Noel felt as if she had gotten him into a jam. The big day, the reporter explained, was not the November election day, but rather Noel's upcoming wedding to the mother of his seven-year-old daughter. As she put the paper down, Ryla looked regretful. "I'm so sorry for this, Noel. I had no idea that the reporter would take a seven-year-old's word concerning us getting married."

"It didn't help matters when you went all no-comment on them."

A waiter arrived at the table with the dinner menus. After looking them over for a minute, Ryla ordered the grass-fed Texas beef tenderloin with crispy rock shrimp.

Noel ordered the USDA prime bone-in cowboy rib eye with red-chili onion rings.

When the waiter walked away, Ryla broached the subject again. "You can't blame me for everything, Noel. I told you that bringing Jaylen on the campaign trail was a bad idea."

"You didn't tell me that you would throw me under the bus when I needed you to take a stand," Noel threw back at her.

"What did you want me to do? Tell those reporters that my daughter was nothing more than a little liar, while she stood with such hope in her eyes?"

Even though he didn't want to admit it, Noel understood Ryla's dilemma. He hadn't wanted to hurt Jaylen, either. He had also chosen to walk away without setting the reporters straight. Noel held up a hand. "Whether you are responsible for not clearing up the matter, or whether I'm responsible for insisting that she be here with me in the first place, we can debate all night long. But right now I'm in a jam, and I need your help to get out of it."

"My help? What can I do?"

Before Noel could answer, the waiter returned with their dinner. He sat the plates before them, and both Noel and Ryla moaned at the rich aromas that drifted upward. Noel grabbed Ryla's hands and prayed over the food.

When he was finished praying, Ryla smiled and said, "This is new."

"What, the praying?" Noel asked.

"Yes. When we were in college, you'd start wolfing down your food the moment it hit the table," she said with a slight giggle.

"Hey, I was a growing boy. And I was always on the court. I needed to eat in order to keep my stamina up," he protested.

"Admit it, Noel, you were just greedy, with no home training." She was still smiling as she needled him.

Placing his fork on his plate, he said, "All right, maybe I didn't have much home training then. But my brother taught me the value of prayer a few years back, so I like to pray over my food . . . if that's okay with you."

"Perfect." Ryla picked up her fork and knife and began cutting into her meal. After taking the first bite, she savored it a moment by closing her eyes, then said, "Delicious."

"I'm glad you like it," Noel said after he realized that he had been holding his breath, staring at Ryla, waiting for her to acknowledge whether she liked the food. He really didn't know why it mattered to him, except that he liked the restaurant and wanted to share the experience with her.

They ate the rest of their meals in silence. But once Noel had wiped his mouth and put his napkin down for the last time, he turned back to Ryla and admitted, "My poll numbers are down. I could lose the election over this."

Ryla put her napkin on the plate. "I'm sorry to hear that. I know this election means a lot to you."

"Jaylen means much more. So, I don't want you to think that I regret having her in my life."

Ryla nodded. "I know that, Noel. All anyone has to do is be around the two of you for a minute and they would notice the love you and Jaylen have for one another." She lowered her head for a moment. When she faced him again, she said, "Sometimes I feel so guilty for how long I kept you and Jaylen apart. And . . . and, I'm truly sorry for that." She let out a slow, bitter laugh. "I seem to be sorry for a lot of things lately."

He didn't know what had put Ryla in this mood, but she was right where he wanted her to be. So, he went all-in. "You know, if you're really, truly sorry, you can help me with my little situation."

"How can I help you, Noel?"

He leaned in to get closer and put his hand over hers as he said, "Marry me."

CHAPTER 10

If Noel hadn't been holding her hand, Ryla would have fallen out of her seat. "What did you just say?"

"I asked you to marry me."

"But, Noel, you've been so angry with me about Jaylen. I — I'm a little surprised that you would even entertain the thought of marriage right now." Although Ryla was surprised, her heart was beating a mile a minute and she felt butterflies floating about her stomach. In the dreams she'd had of Noel popping the question, he'd always been on bended knee, but holding hands was just as good, Ryla told herself.

Noel said, "I'm not thinking that we have to really get married. So, I guess I'm asking for you to be engaged to me for a little while."

And just that quickly, the dream died. She pulled her hands away from him. "What?"

"Look, if I don't do something drastic, I

could lose this election. So I was hoping that you would be willing to pretend to be engaged to me for a while."

"So, we wouldn't have to get married?" she asked to clarify the situation.

As if he was in a business meeting, he leaned back in his seat and with that I-rule-the-world air that he had as he told her of his plan. "This is the way I was thinking we'd play this thing out . . . The election is in three months. So, if we had a quick engagement and then arranged a late-September wedding —"

"But I thought you didn't want us to get married," Ryla interrupted.

"Woman, will you let me finish?"

With a wave of her hand, she indicated the floor was his.

"As I was saying." He gave her a pointed look, daring her to interrupt him again. "We'll plan the wedding for late September, sometime around the twenty-fourth. We'll do it up, invite our family and friends, and then as I am standing in front of the preacher waiting for you to recite your vows, you scream something like 'I just can't do this,' and then run out of the church like somebody just snatched your purse and you're trying to get it back."

"I'm not about to humiliate myself just so

you can get the sympathy vote," Ryla protested.

Noel appeared to be puzzled as he said, "I don't understand you, Ryla. You've been running in and out of my life since the day I met you, and now that I'm asking you to do what you are obviously good at, to help me, you act like it's a cardinal sin."

Okay, Ryla could admit that Noel had probably received the short end of the stick when he decided to date her back in college. But couldn't he see that asking her to become a runaway bride was just as bad as what she had done to him? "This is not right."

"My career is on the line, Ryla." He pointed at the newspaper. "The press has practically married us off already. I can't go back and say that we're not getting married. Do you know how bad it would look if I tell my constituents that I'm not willing to marry the mother of my child?"

"Well, we could just get married for real, you know," Ryla suggested. But when she saw the look of horror on Noel's face, she realized that she had been right about his feelings toward her. Before she could stop herself, she belted out, "Do you really hate me that much, Noel?"

Noel shook his head. "I don't hate you,

Ryla. But I don't trust you, either."

She understood why he didn't trust her. If he had taken Jaylen away from her and kept her for seven years, she would have a hard time believing a word he said, too. "What I did may not have been right, but I had my reasons."

He harrumphed. "I figured out what your so-called reason was. And that was no reason at all."

"How can you sit here and even think that I would have been fine staying with a man who cheated on me?"

"I never cheated on you." Noel's voice roared throughout the room. Heads swiveled. He took a sip of his iced tea and then continued in a lower voice. "Cathy tried to kiss me. That much is true, but if you hadn't run off, you would have seen that I politely took her arms from around my neck and told her that I was in love with you."

Oh, my God, was Noel right? Had she run off too soon? If so, that was one more thing Ryla would blame on her father. She must have inherited her running gene from him. "You're right, Noel. I left as soon as she kissed you. I thought she was doing what you wanted her to do." Ryla shook her head. She no longer felt butterflies fluttering in her stomach. She felt plain ill. "I have wished a thousand times that I could go back and make all of this right."

"It's too late now."

"It's never too late, Noel. Not if we're willing to give it a try."

"Some things are too hard to forgive, Ryla."

Ryla saw the look of sorrow in Noel's eye as he admitted that he hadn't yet forgiven her for what she'd done. But she was also encouraged by the fact that Noel had just admitted that he had been in love with her in college. Sure, she had messed up. But Ryla wasn't ready to throw in the towel so easily this time. Noel wanted her to pretend to marry him, and now that she knew for sure that Noel wasn't a cheater, she wanted nothing more than to marry him. Maybe this was her chance to make things right between them.

She leaned over a bit and took Noel's hand in hers. "Okay, I'll do it. I'll marry you."

He removed his hand. "You mean, you'll pretend to marry me, right?"

She smiled. Noel wanted a runaway bride, but little did he know Ryla's running days were over. "I just have one question," she said, ignoring his question.

"What's that?"

"Where's my engagement ring?"

He popped himself on the forehead with the palm of his hand. "I'm so sorry, Ryla. I didn't even think to pick up a ring."

She frowned. "Well, I'll tell you right now, Noel Carter, I'm not about to get engaged to anyone who doesn't even bother to buy me a ring."

"You got it, Ryla. I'll take care of it first thing in the morning."

She looked him square in the face and said, "I don't want you to delegate this to one of your staff members. I'm not marrying any man who won't even take the time to find his fiancé an engagement ring."

"I'll get the ring. But don't you think you need to calm down a bit? I mean, we're only pretending, remember?"

"I don't care. I've never been engaged before, so if you want me to walk away at the altar, then I want you to treat me like a fiancé throughout the entire engagement. Got it?"

"Got it," Noel said as he lifted a hand to the waiter to get the check.

Ryla had a hard time getting to sleep that night. She didn't feel good about her decision to trick Noel into marrying her. She just hoped that by the end of the engagement, he would be in love with her again and would want to marry her for real, just as much as she wanted to marry him.

Whenever Ryla had a dilemma that she just couldn't see her way through, she called on her girls, Danetta Windham and Surry McDaniel. Jaylen was spending the day with her aunt, going to museums, lunch and then a movie. So Ryla picked up the phone and called Danetta. When Danetta answered, Ryla said, "I know it's early and I apologize if you're not up yet."

Yawning, Danetta said, "I'm getting up. Why are you calling so early on a Saturday morning?"

"I tossed and turned all night long. I really need to talk to you and Surry today. Do you think you can meet me for a late breakfast or early lunch?"

"This sounds serious. Let me get Surry on the phone," Danetta said and then clicked to her other line. When she came back on the line with Ryla, she said, "Okay, Surry is on the line with us."

"What's going on, girl? Why are you up at this ungodly hour?" Surry asked.

"It's seven in the morning. You two are acting like I called at four in the morning. Where is the sisterhood here? I really need your help."

After razzing her for a few more minutes, Danetta and Surry agreed to meet up with Ryla in Fort Hood, a military town that was just about the halfway point between Houston and Dallas.

They met at one of the local eateries. After hugs and small talk, Ryla began spilling her guts. "I just don't know what to do," Ryla confessed. "The man hates me, but the more time I spend with him, I know for a fact that I never stopped loving him."

Surry was the first to speak. Out of the three of them, she was the more no-nonsense, reality-based kind of girl. She gave and she took, but preferred taking and didn't apologize for it. "So you're saying that this joker asked you to marry him, but not really?"

"He wants me to walk to the altar and then reject him in front of everyone. He's got it in his head that if he refuses to marry me now, he'll be perceived as some despicable man who refused to marry the mother of his child. Coupled with the fact that he hasn't paid child support in the last seven years, Noel thinks the media will have a field day with all the deadbeat dad headlines," Ryla admitted to her friends.

Danetta chimed in. "Advertising is my business, so I can't say that Noel is wrong for considering how it would play out if he refused to marry you after basically letting it be known that he planned to do just that." Danetta picked up her glass of water and sipped. "But you're just starting an event-planning business. Has he thought about your image and what this arrangement could do to your career?"

"No, Noel is hoping that he'll just be thought of as some poor, wronged-again dupe," Ryla said. And for the first time since her conversation with Noel, rather than feeling sorry for herself, she was beginning to get angry.

"He better be careful with that," Surry said. "While some people will feel sorry for the way he was jilted at the altar, there are also people like me, who will think he got what he deserved for being a chump."

"Come on, Surry, how can loving someone make you a chump?" Danetta asked.

Ryla smiled at Danetta's question. Out of the three of them, Danetta was the one who believed in love eternal. After all, she had loved Marshall Windham for ten years before he fell in love with her. The two of them were now married and Danetta believed that the same could happen for all women.

"So are you saying that all the men who

fall in love with you are chumps? And that they haven't bothered to get to know who you are, but rather fall for your beauty?" Ryla asked.

"Exactly," Surry exclaimed as she pushed the bread basket on the table to the far side. "None of them know me at all, and that's why I haven't fallen for any of them."

"Well, Noel knows me. And I guess that's why he doesn't really want to marry me," Ryla said.

"I'm tired of listening to you put yourself down," Danetta said and then added, "I'm not saying that you handled this situation the right way, but you're a good person, Ryla Evans. Any man would be blessed to have you, so remember that."

Ryla nodded. "Okay. Now, will the two of you please be my bridesmaids?"

"Girl, please, I'm not willing to be a part of some sham wedding that is sure to make the news. I'm just getting my business off the ground and I'm currently in talks to two major retailers," Surry told her.

"What?" Danetta almost screamed. "You didn't tell us that your business was expanding." Danetta lifted her hand and she and Surry high-fived.

"I wanted to keep it close to the vest until I was sure the deal would go through,"

Surry told Danetta, and then turned to Ryla. "So, as much as I would love to help with this little sham wedding, I can't risk the bad publicity right now."

Surry designed African attire and sold her sundresses and accessories in little boutiques in about five different states. "You're a true friend, Surry," Ryla said sarcastically. "But you won't have to worry about this wedding ending up on CNN because Noel Carter got ditched by his deranged baby mama."

Danetta squinted as she looked at Ryla. "Okay, you're up to something. I can tell by the way you're grinning."

"I think I remember you grinning quite a bit when you were engaged, so don't act like I'm doing anything out of the ordinary," Ryla said to Danetta.

"Yeah, but she was engaged for real. This clown you're with wants you to pretend." Surry shook her head in disgust. "And they wonder why nobody trusts politicians anymore."

Ryla didn't respond, but Danetta pointed at her again. "See, that's the grin I'm talking about. Tell us what you've got up your sleeve right now, Ryla Evans, or I'm not showing up at this wedding."

"Okay, okay." Ryla held up a hand. "It's

simple, really. Noel and I would be married already if I hadn't left college and refused to talk to him. So, all I'm doing now is righting a wrong that I did to Noel and Jaylen.

"You see," Ryla continued, "I don't plan on doing a thing the way Noel wants. Which should come as no surprise to him or anyone else who knows me."

Surry nodded, with a slight smirk on her face. "What are you going to do?"

"I'm going to marry him."

Danetta looked from Surry and then back to Ryla and said, "You can't do that. The man doesn't want to be married."

"Noel loves me . . . or at least he loved me at one time. I just need to show him that we are meant to be together. If I hadn't run off years ago, we would already be married anyway, so what's the difference."

"I'm with Danetta on this one," Surry said. "You can't just marry someone who doesn't want to be married. This thing could backfire on you big-time."

"Well, I'm desperate and I need your help. So, if you don't mind, I'd appreciate it if the two of you would stop talking all doom and gloom. Help me figure out a way to get Noel to fall back in love with me so he'll want me to say 'I do' for real. Got it?"

Surry snapped her finger. "I think I know what you should do."

"Spill it," Ryla said, looking as anxious as a high school girl waiting on her first date to knock on her door.

Surry leaned forward in her seat. "You're not getting married until September, so you've got two and a half months to make this work."

"Go on," Ryla urged.

"You simply tell Noel that to make the engagement look real, he needs to act like he's a man in love. Tell him to plan a few dates for you and to hold your hand in public. Things like that."

Danetta sat silently shaking her head.

"How is that going to change anything?" Ryla asked.

"Girl, you know how to work it." Surry snapped her finger again, but this time she added a little attitude with it. "Make that man see what he's missing by not having you in his life. Every time you go out with him, you need to be dressed so fine that his mouth starts watering."

"I'm going to pray for y'all," Danetta said with a slight giggle.

Ryla pointed at her. "You're laughing because you know that's how you landed Marshall."

Danetta shook her head. "I didn't trick Marshall into marrying me."

"No, but you changed the game when you changed your wardrobe. Remember how it drove Marshall insane to watch you go out on dates with other men while dressed so sexy?" Ryla nudged Danetta.

Danetta looked as if she was pondering Ryla's last statement for a moment and then she asked, "And you're sure that Noel was in love with you once?"

"He told me so himself!"

Danetta leaned forward and said, "Okay, well, since your wardrobe is already pretty well put together, I suggest that you change that attitude of yours."

Hands on hips. "What's wrong with my attitude?"

"Here me out," Danetta said. "All I'm saying is Noel is probably expecting you to give him nothing but attitude, since he forced you to bring Jaylen to Dallas and is now practically forcing you to get him out of a predicament by doing something that will ultimately make you look bad. So, change the game by being sweet and loving."

"I like it. Thank you both for your help," Ryla said to Danetta and Surry. The three women then finished their meals and walked out of the restaurant.

Ryla headed back to Dallas with her mind set on getting her man back.

CHAPTER 11

"Where have you been?" Noel's voice thundered through Ryla's aunt's house the moment she walked through the door. He had driven to her place first thing that morning to ask if she wanted to go with him to pick out her ring. But neither she nor anyone else had been home at that time. He decided to go ahead and pick the ring out himself and then bring it back to Ryla. But when he arrived back at the house in the late afternoon, Jaylen opened the door and informed him that her mother wasn't home yet.

Jaylen ran to Ryla, and there was excitement in her voice as she said, "Daddy has been waiting for you."

"For hours," Noel added as he came and stood with them.

"Well, I hope I'm worth the wait," Ryla said to Noel as she bent down and gave Jaylen a kiss on the cheek. "And I hope you had fun with Auntie Shelly today."

"Oh, I did. Auntie Shelly is the best." Jaylen was smiling from ear to ear.

Noel picked her up and put her on his shoulder as they walked into the parlor. "I'm glad you had fun with your aunt. I would have loved to take you to the movies, but your mommy sent Daddy on an all-day errand."

Aunt Shelly was sitting in the parlor. She gave Ryla a playful swat on the behind as she passed by her and then said, "Why on earth would you keep this man waiting on you for so long?"

"I was having lunch with some of my friends, Auntie, I didn't even know he was here."

Aunt Shelly stood as Noel put Jaylen down. She grabbed her hand and said, "I'll take Jaylen upstairs so you and Noel can have a chat." Aunt Shelly winked at Ryla as she headed out of the room.

Ryla grabbed hold of Noel's arm. "Did you get my ring?"

Noel patted the pocket of his suit jacket. "Let me hand it to you."

Horror-stricken, Ryla said, "Noel Carter, you'll do no such thing."

Shaking his head, Noel said, "I seriously don't understand you. You asked me to get you a ring. So I went and got it. Now you

119

don't want me to give it to you?"

Ryla plopped down on the high-back chair next to the sofa. "Men," she said with exasperation in her voice. "I've never been engaged before, Noel. So, I don't just want you to take the ring out of your pocket and hand it to me. I want you to propose."

"I did that last night."

Ryla hit him with both barrels. "Don't you want Jaylen to know how a man is supposed to propose to the woman he loves and wants to marry?"

This was all a bit much for Noel. He'd done everything she'd asked of him, but even that wasn't good enough for Ryla. Now she wanted him to perform. He was about to decline from partaking in this spectacle, but then he realized that this could be a teaching moment for his daughter. He would never want her to marry a man who just handed her a ring without much thought. "I'll be right back," he said, and then swung around to leave.

Ryla jumped up and grabbed his arm again. "Where are you going? I thought you had something for me?"

"I do, but you have a point. I should do this right. I'll be back in an hour."

As Noel made his way out of the house, he looked down at his attire and couldn't believe that he'd worn a Nike jogging suit to propose to Ryla. What was he thinking?

He rushed home and changed into a tailored charcoal-gray two-piece suit with a lavender shirt and a lavender, gray and black tie. Noel then made his way to Mockingbird Florist on East Mockingbird Lane. His first thought was to purchase a dozen red roses, but that seemed too cliché. So, he purchased the dozen, but then asked for the petals without the stems on ten of the red roses. The florist handed him the two stemmed roses that were still intact and then gave him the petals in a clear plastic bag.

Having everything that he needed to make this a memorable moment for Ryla and Jaylen, Noel got in his car and sped back to Ryla's place. Before announcing his presence, he opened his bag of petals and sprinkled them on the porch and the three steps that led to the door. Noel then rang the doorbell and waited.

Jaylen was the first one to the door. She opened it with a huge grin on her face. "Daddy, you came back!"

"Of course I did, sweetheart. You can always count on your daddy to keep his word." He handed his daughter one of the roses and said, "That's for you, baby girl. I'm the first man who ever gave you a rose, but I sure won't be the last."

Jaylen inhaled the fragrance and then looked back to her father with so much joy in her eyes that it nearly made him weak.

"Thank you, Daddy. And if some man wants to give me a rose when I get older, I'll be sure to tell him that my daddy did it first."

Ryla and Shelly came up behind Jaylen and pulled the door open. Ryla stepped onto the porch while Aunt Shelly leaned against the door frame. "What did you do first?" Ryla asked Noel as she looked around at the rose petals all over the porch.

"This," he said as he handed her the other red rose. He then took her hand, walked her across the rose petal-laden porch and got down on his knee. He pulled a three-carat princess-cut diamond ring with a white-gold band and the Tiffany & Co. inscription on the inner side of the ring.

Ryla gasped as tears ran down her face.

Her tears caught him off guard and made him want to make this moment even more special for her. He kissed the hand he was holding, and then glanced up at her as he said, "Ryla Evans, would you do me the honor of m-marrying me?" He fumbled a bit, but it wasn't every day that a man asked a woman to marry him.

Ryla squealed, jumped up and down and then fell into Noel's arms. "Of course I'll marry you."

Noel was holding on to Ryla feeling pretty good about pulling off a proposal that brought tears to her eyes, when Jaylen jumped onto his back and screamed, "Thanks for marrying my mommy."

Aunt Shelly ran down the porch and hugged Ryla. "Let me see that ring, girl."

As Ryla showed off her ring to Aunt Shelly, Noel was brought back to reality. This wasn't some reality show with a script, where everyone knew where they were supposed to be and what type of drama they were supposed to bring with them. Jaylen was his daughter, and he had an obligation to bring her happiness and do no wrong.

Ryla waved her hand in front of him, indicating that he should place the ring on her finger.

She was so excited that Noel could tell she had gotten swept away in the moment also. Neither of them had thought very much about how all this would affect Jaylen, but they needed to talk about it very soon. He slipped the ring on her finger, and then helped Jaylen down from her spot on his back. As Noel stood, he grabbed Ryla's hand and stared at the ring. It was beautiful, as if the designer had Ryla in mind when he'd made this particular ring.

He covered her hand with his own as he stood and pulled her close to him. Their lips were so close they touched as he said, "We need to talk."

Talk? Ryla didn't want to waste time talking. She wanted to wrap her arms around Noel and kiss him as he whispered words of love in her ear.

"Come on," he said as he pulled her back toward the parlor. Jaylen and Aunt Shelly followed behind. But Noel turned to Jaylen and said, "Honey, Daddy needs to speak with Mommy alone. Do you mind going to your room for a few minutes?"

"Okay," Jaylen said, and then skipped out of the room as if she was the happiest little girl in the world.

Aunt Shelly stretched and yawned. "I think I'll go to bed and give you two some privacy." She hugged Ryla again and then hugged Noel. "Welcome to the family," she said with joy, and then headed to her bedroom.

"I think we've made a mistake," Noel said as soon as they were alone.

Ryla was looking at her ring when Noel said those words. But she quickly put her hand down and gave him a what-you-talking-'bout-Willis stare.

"I didn't think about how all of this would affect Jaylen when I asked you to do this for me."

"Jaylen will be fine." *Once we're married,* she wanted to add, but left that part of the conversation in her head.

Pacing the room, Noel said, "I don't know about this. I really don't want to hurt Jaylen any more than I have already by not being around."

If Ryla was truthful with herself, she would admit that she hadn't thought much about how this would affect Jaylen if things didn't turn out the way she planned. Her daughter would be crushed. But she was the one who pushed Noel out of their life, so now she had to do everything in her power to bring him back. She sat down on the couch and held out a hand to Noel. "Come sit next to me."

Noel kept pacing.

She got up, walked over to him, grabbed his hand and walked him over to the couch, then said, "Sit."

Noel sat down and admitted, "I was angry and I blamed you for my poll numbers dropping. But I was the one who forced you to bring Jaylen to Dallas while I was in the middle of a campaign. So, if this fiasco is anyone's fault, it's mine."

"It's not your fault that I kept Jaylen away from you." She caressed his hand. "I want to help you win this election. . . . Let me help you, Noel." She wanted to say, "Let's just go all the way and get married," but she hadn't forgotten the look of horror on his face when she'd asked about that the previous night.

"Maybe I should just run my race and not worry so much about what the reporters are saying about my personal life."

"Even President Obama once gave a speech while running when the whole Reverend Wright issue wouldn't go away. So, I really think we need to stick to your original plan." *Please, please, please stick to the plan,* she silently begged. "Jaylen and I will be fine."

"Are you sure about this, Ryla? I mean, I don't want my ambitions to negatively affect Jaylen."

"Believe me, Jaylen couldn't be prouder of you. She wants you to win this election just as much as I do."

He sat there for a moment. Then as he took a deep breath, he turned to her and said, "If you're sure . . . Ian has scheduled a meet and greet with some potential campaign donors. The press will be at the event and he'd like for us to announce our engagement at that time."

"That's fine, but I need to make sure you understand my expectations."

He gave her a don't-start-no-mess look and then asked, "Your expectations?"

Ryla lifted a hand. "Calm down. I'm not asking for alimony or anything like that," she joked.

"Okay, so what do you want?"

"Well, if we are going to convince people that we have fallen in love again and that's why we've decided to get married, we need to do a few things to make it look real."

"Like what?" Noel sounded skeptical.

"For one thing, I think you should take me out on a few dates."

Noel laughed. "In case you missed it, I am in the middle of running for the U.S. Congress."

"A man in love would make the time," Ryla chided.

"But a man on a mission wouldn't have the time for love. And people would understand that I'm busy and don't have time for anything but campaigning."

Ryla folded her arms. "I wouldn't understand, so I suggest you find the time to wine and dine me, Mr. I-Need-a-Wife."

"A fake wife," he reminded her.

"Whatever."

After putting Jaylen to bed, Ryla sat on the edge of her bed staring at the princess-cut ring on her finger. After leaving Noel, she had given up on the idea of ever finding someone to marry. Men were just too unpredictable. One minute they were in love and the next they were cheating.

Ryla had convinced herself that she didn't need or want the unpredictable life that falling in love would bring. But now that Noel was back, and now that she knew for sure that he hadn't cheated on her with Cathy, she was ready to move forward.

Lying down in her bed, Ryla still couldn't take her eyes off her ring. She chided herself for being silly and then reached over to turn the light on her nightstand off. That was when her cell phone rang. Glancing at her caller ID, Ryla saw that her mother was calling.

She smiled as she answered the phone, because she couldn't believe that she'd totally forgotten to call her mother and tell her the good news. "Hey, Mom, have I got news for you."

"And I have news for you also," Juanita told her.

Tamping down her excitement, Ryla said, "Okay, you first."

"Well, I just thought you'd want to know that I signed two new clients for you today."

Ryla sat back up. "You're kidding. Who . . . What kind of event do they want?"

"One wants a sweet sixteen party for his daughter and the other wants you to plan their engagement party. Both parties are six months out, so I just need to know when you'll be back home so I can set up a meeting with the clients."

Ryla glanced at her ring and smiled. "I don't know, Mom, I may have to move my event-planning business to Dallas."

"What? Are you telling me that you'd rather be there with Shelly than back in Houston with your mom?"

Ryla wanted to drag her news out, make her mother sweat a little while, but she was so excited about the possibility of getting married to Noel that she couldn't hold it in. So she blurted out, "Noel just asked me to marry him. He gave me a beautiful princess-cut diamond ring."

There was silence on the line for a moment and then Juanita said, "But what about all those women who came out of the woodwork talking about how they used to date him?"

"Mom, Noel and I haven't been together in eight years — of course he's dated other women. I'm not worried about them."

"But I thought you told me he was a cheater?"

She had brought this on herself, with her mistrust and quick judgments. Now she would have to fix things or her mother would forever see Noel as something he wasn't. "I was wrong. Noel never cheated on me. I left him before figuring out what really happened."

"I guess your father and I are to blame for that." The sound of Juanita's voice held regret.

Ryla could have spent all night long explaining to her mother just how much her mother and father had cost her, but she wasn't going there. Juanita Evans-Berkley was a wonderful woman; the fact that in a lineup of one loser and six good men, her mother would pick the loser every time had nothing to do with the love she had for her mother. "I don't want to think about things like that now, I just want to enjoy this moment and be happy." She also wanted Noel to marry her for real, but she was keeping that little secret to herself.

CHAPTER 12

"She wants me to take her out on dates," Noel told Ian as he walked into his office.

"Isn't that what a man does for the woman he loves?" Ian asked with a noticeable smirk on his face.

"Don't be cute," Noel said as he flopped into his napa leather office chair. He kicked his feet up onto his desk. "That woman is driving me crazy. First she demands an engagement ring, and then she tells me that I couldn't just hand it to her."

"So you got all romantic with it, huh?"

Bragging a bit, Noel said, "You know how I do it." He stood and started strutting around the room. "I put rose petals on the porch and the steps, and then I rang the doorbell. I handed both Jaylen and Ryla a single red rose when they opened the door."

As if remembering something he'd forgotten to do, Noel walked over to the file cabinet, grabbed a folder and then went back to his chair.

"Don't keep a brother waiting. What did you do after that?" Ian asked.

Noel sat down as he looked through the file folder.

"Was the proposal *that* bad for you?" Ian continued waiting for Noel to respond.

"Huh?" Noel glanced up, and then shook his head. "Actually, I enjoyed every minute of it. That is, until my daughter jumped on my back and thanked me for marrying her mother."

"What could be so wrong with that?"

Noel hadn't yet revealed his plan to have Ryla leave him at the altar to Ian. Since the man was his campaign manager, Noel felt that he owed him the truth. "Sit down, Ian. I have something to tell you that you're not going to like."

Noel spent the next few minutes clueing Ian in on his runaway bride plan. When he was finished, Ian said, "Do you know how many marriages of convenience there are in the political spectrum? Why can't you just marry the girl and let her move back to Houston?"

"I can't do that, Ian. Not even to win an election."

Ian shook his head. "I think you're making a mistake. You're counting on your constituents giving you the pity vote, but some of them may just assume that Ryla had good reason for not marrying you."

"And some of them will feel as if I'm free of a woman who could keep a child from me for seven years." Noel opened the file he needed to review and began going over information his staff had compiled on some of the campaign donors that would be attending the luncheon today.

Ian sighed as he sat down in the seat in front of Noel's desk. "You really need to let go of this bitterness you have against Ryla. She seems like a nice woman, and if you want my opinion, I think she's still in love with you."

Noel glanced up and then pointed at the file he was studying. "Are you sure that David Lewis will be attending the luncheon today?"

"He confirmed last week, so I believe he'll be there." Ian leaned forward and asked, "Did we just change the subject?"

Noel closed the file and stared at Ian. "Shouldn't you be happy that I have my mind on the campaign?"

Ian held up a hand. "Don't get me wrong. I'm glad that you're all-in when it comes to your campaign. I just don't want you to forget about the issue that is dogging us at the moment."

"That issue being . . . ?" Noel asked, in a sarcastic tone.

Before Ian could answer, there was a gentle knock on the door and then it opened with Ryla and Jaylen peering in. "Is this a good time?" Ryla asked.

Ian jumped up, with a big smile on his face. "Come on in." As Ryla and Jaylen walked in, he added, "I hear that congratulations are in order."

"Show him your ring, Mom," Jaylen said as she grabbed Ryla's left hand.

Ryla held up her ring finger. "Thank you, I was really surprised with the ring that Noel had chosen. It is absolutely gorgeous."

Beautiful was the word Noel was thinking of as he watched Ryla show off her engagement ring. Her makeup was flawless, but if Ryla wore no makeup at all she would still be lovely. It irritated him that he was attracted to her, so instead he gruffly said, "You're early."

Ryla glanced at her watch. "I thought you said the luncheon begins at eleven?"

"It does. And you made it here at the perfect time. Now you can ride with us to the event," Ian interrupted.

Noel stood and approached them. Ian was butting in, trying to smooth things over with

Ryla for him, but he didn't ask for any help. Jaylen ran to her father and he picked her up. "Hey, pumpkin, how are you doing today?"

"I'm great. Mommy says I get to be the flower girl."

"I can't think of anyone who'd do a better job than you, pumpkin."

"I'm going to sprinkle rose petals on the floor for Mommy, just like you did."

Noel drifted back to Saturday night when he got down on bended knee and watched tears roll down Ryla's face as she accepted his proposal. The memory softened him as he spoke to Ryla again.

Noel put Jaylen down and then said to Ryla, "Thank you for helping me with this luncheon. And I'm glad you're early enough to ride over with me."

Ryla put her arm around Jaylen. "Well, it looks like I'll always need to bring you with me when I have to deal with your daddy. You seem to put him in a good mood instantly."

Noel lovingly pinched Jaylen's cheeks. "Of course my little girl puts me in a good mood."

"I'm your good-mood charm, huh, Daddy?"

Noel liked the sound of that. He had been

disgruntled about so many things in life for way too long. Now that he was putting his life back on track, he needed a good mood charm to help him remember to smile and be thankful for the little things. "Yeah, baby girl, you're definitely my good-mood charm. I'm just hoping that our donors will throw me some good moods today."

"We really need a boost in our fundraiser to combat some of these negative attacks that your opponent has been airing," Ian said, looking slightly worried.

"I don't know how many times I have to tell you to stop worrying. I got this," Noel said as he strutted out of the office with his two special ladies by his side.

The luncheon was held at the Hilton and was five-star all the way. Ryla stood by Noel's side as he shook hands and rubbed elbows with constituents and big-money donors who didn't even live in Texas. As she worked the room with him, Ryla found herself reminiscing on their college days. Even back then, Noel had known that he was destined to not just be somebody, but be that somebody who looked back, and helped the next one in line.

"Basketball isn't my only dream," Noel had

told her while dribbling the ball that was never far from him. "I want to do something big. Something that's not only about me, but that will help other people."

"You're so good at basketball, I'd never imagine that you would ever want to do anything else," Ryla had said with the stardust of love and adoration in her eyes.

"Yeah, baby." Dribble. Shoot. Swish. As the ball bounced back to him, he said, "With this ball in my hand, people stop and take notice. But one day, they're going to notice me for a different reason." He came and sat next to her on the bleachers. "I want other people to have the opportunity to become successful, too. I mean, I feel that I'm destined for greatness, but what about the people who can't dribble and shoot like I can? What about the people in my old neighborhood who can't afford a college education?"

"What do you think you can do to help them?"

"Well, I don't know just yet, but I think about this kind of stuff all the time, you know."

Noel scooted closer to her and looked into her eyes, and Ryla saw how serious he was about his dreams. It made her wish that she hadn't grown up so spoiled and sheltered.

"My brother says that God has already given us everything we need to succeed," Noel continued. "And if that is true, then once I'm done with basketball, I'm going to find a way to help thousands of people."

"Wow" was all she could say, because she was so amazed that a guy with the potential that Noel had would even take time out of his day to worry about those less fortunate than him. He was truly a prince among men, and he was all hers.

At least Ryla had thought Noel was all hers at that time, until she had let Cathy drive her away from the only man she'd ever loved. But that was then and this was now. She looked up as Noel stood at the podium addressing his five-hundred-dollar-a-plate listeners.

"I want to thank you all for coming here this afternoon to show your support for my candidacy. I have dreamed about the day that my life would be used to help others, and because of your generosity, that day seems ever closer." Noel glanced at Ryla, who sat on the right side of the podium with Jaylen seated next to her.

He turned back to his constituents and said, "And I guess it's high time that I introduce you all to another dream of mine." He held out his hand to her. "Ryla, baby, come up here so I can introduce you to everyone."

He called me baby. She stood and walked over to him as if she was in a Miss America pageant and knew she was about to win the thing. He squeezed her left hand as he told the crowd, "I've been in love with Ryla since we were in college. I let her get away from me back then." He held up her hand so others could see the three carats she wore. He pointed at her finger. "But this time I put a ring on it."

The crowd went wild with applause. Cameramen and reporters ran to the front of the room. So many flashbulbs went off that it blinded Ryla as she leaned into Noel.

"You okay?" he whispered into her ear.

"Too many cameras."

Noel held up a hand. "Okay, fellows, give my bride-to-be a little space. We will take an engagement picture and send it to all of the media outlets." He put his hand over his heart. "I promise."

"When's the big day, Noel?" one of the reporters yelled from the floor.

"September twenty-second."

"I bet your little girl is thrilled about this news, aye, Ryla?" another reporter asked.

"She's even more thrilled about being the flower girl," Ryla said.

"Are you sure you can plan a wedding in

139

just eight weeks, Ryla?" a reporter yelled at them.

"Event planning is what I do for a living. So, eight weeks is plenty of time. Hey, I might even move the date up a few weeks," she joked, and the room broke out in laughter.

Noel leaned down and whispered, "You're a natural at this."

She glanced up at him, and at that moment her heart caught in her throat as their eyes locked. Earlier, in his office, Ryla could have sworn that Noel was angry with her, but right now he was looking at her the way he used to back in the day . . . when she was his and he was hers.

A snarky reporter broke their trance as he asked, "Does the rush have anything to do with the fact that Noel's poll numbers have tanked since he brought you and your daughter on the campaign trail with him?"

Noel's head jolted. "Who asked that?" he demanded.

But before he could get an answer, another reporter said, "Tell us the truth, Ryla, is this some kind of publicity stunt . . . like a marriage of convenience or something?"

Ryla lightly brushed her hand over Noel's two-day stubble and then turned to the reporter and spoke the truth that was in her heart. "I have loved Noel Carter since the moment I laid eyes on him. I would marry him if he wasn't running for public office, so I can honestly say that our marriage will be one filled with love, honor and respect."

The audience applauded again. Ryla started to walk back to her seat, but Noel surprised her by leaning over and laying a soft, moist kiss on her lips.

"Thank you, baby," Noel said, and then turned back to his constituents to deliver his speech.

Ryla prayed that her wobbly legs would carry her back to her chair. It didn't make sense how out of sorts she was over a quick, soft, wet kiss. She sat down and closed her eyes as she wondered if she was strong enough for the game she was playing. Because if Noel didn't fall in love with her as she hoped, Ryla knew without a doubt that her world would fall apart.

CHAPTER 13

Noel was so pleased with Ryla's performance that he would have taken her out that night even if she hadn't already made dates a condition of their engagement. He was dressed in his best tux as he drove to Ryla's aunt's place. He knew a friend who had a friend who worked for the Dallas Symphony Orchestra. So, Noel spent the afternoon tracking his friend down in order to get tickets to tonight's sold-out performance.

When he called Ryla and informed her that they were going to Morton H. Meyerson Symphony Center and afterward to a quaint little place in Oak Cliff for dinner, she practically squealed her delight.

When Ryla had first insisted that he act like an engaged man and take her out on a few dates, Noel had thought he was entering into the worst eight weeks of his life, but after receiving such an appreciative response from her, Noel began to think that he just might enjoy these next few weeks after all.

Pulling up at her house, Noel tried to prepare himself for how beautiful Ryla was sure to look. The woman would be gorgeous in just a tank top and shorts. And she had impeccable taste in clothes, so he was a little worried that he would experience another jaw-dropping moment when she opened the door. *It's just Ryla, so calm down,* he told himself as he rang the doorbell.

But when Ryla opened the door dressed in a navy blue strapless evening gown that flowed all the way to the floor, his heart almost stopped. Her hair was pinned up with a few curls dangling against her neck. He wanted to grasp her sweet face and pull her against him. But instead he instructed his body to calm itself. "You're beautiful," he told her as she stepped onto the porch.

"What? No rose petals tonight?" She grinned as she teased him.

"I try to only use rose petals when I'm getting down on my knee to ask a woman to marry me."

"Is that a fact?"

"Them be the facts, ma'am." They walked down the steps and Noel opened the car door for her and waited while she situated herself. He then closed the door and jumped into the driver's side of the car and drove off.

"Thanks for taking me to the symphony, Noel. I've never watched a symphony perform, so this will be a real treat."

He was surprised by her statement. Because as far as Noel was concerned, a woman as beautiful as Ryla should be treated to the finer things of life every day of the week. If she had truly belonged to him, Noel would make it his business to make her feel like a princess. But Noel forced himself to remember that Ryla no longer belonged to him.

The best seats that Noel could obtain for tonight's performance were in the balcony. Noel wasn't worried about the balcony seats, though. Even though the symphony center seated a little over two thousand people, it was well known for its high acoustical quality. "Are these seats okay for you? They were the best I could do at such short notice."

"Are you kidding?" Ryla asked in awe-struck amazement. "I prefer the balcony. I can see everything that happens on the stage from here."

He relaxed in his seat as the show started but found himself watching Ryla more than the orchestra. He couldn't take his eyes off her for more than a minute at a time, for fear that he would miss one of her delightful, wonder-struck expressions as the symphony struck cords that seemed to come straight from heaven.

Ryla caught him watching her and said, "Watch the show."

"I am" was all Noel said, but kept right on watching her enjoy the symphony. When it was over, they drove to Oak Cliff for dinner.

Ryla said, "You know, I have to ask . . ." Ryla turned toward him.

"What?"

"After taking me to a fabulous symphony in the heart of the downtown area, with all sorts of restaurants close by . . . why on earth would you drive me to Oak Cliff?" She leaned back, studied him for a moment and then said, "Are you trying to get the sympathy vote for being carjacked too?"

Laughing, Noel shook his head. "I grew up in Oak Cliff. It might be a little rough around the edges, but there are plenty of good people in my old neighborhood. Some of my constituents are there and, believe it or not, Bolsa, the restaurant I'm taking you to, had been dubbed the best place to take a date by the *Dallas Observer*."

"Best place to take a date, huh?" Ryla

leaned into the luxury of his soft leather seats. "Why is that?"

Noel glanced over at Ryla. She really was beautiful, and he was in trouble if he didn't watch himself. "For one, they have *mmm-mmm,* humming kind of good food. They do drink challenges on Wednesday night."

"Drink challenges? But I thought you stopped drinking years ago," she said.

"Keeping up with my bio, huh?" Noel grinned at her and then said, "But it's not that kind of drink challenge. The customer's give the bartender the ingredients they want in a drink and he has to be able to make the drink taste like something you'd want to drink."

"Sounds like fun. But I'm like you . . . I don't drink. I never acquired a taste for the stuff," Ryla admitted.

"My problem was I developed too much of a taste for the stuff. And it led me down a seriously scary path."

"I heard about the gambling, too," Ryla said almost apologetically.

Noel shrugged. "I did it all. I can't even complain about the stories the tabloids have told about me." His eyes took on a look of gratitude as he thought back to how he pulled himself out of that wild lifestyle. "I'm just so thankful to my brother. Because no

matter what people said about me, no matter what I did back then, he would call me
up and say, 'You are not who they say you
are. You are better than this.' And then one
day, I started to believe him."

"And now you're getting ready to become
a U.S. congressman."

Noel nodded. "If God sees fit." He held
on to the steering wheel with one hand and
grabbed her hand with the other and
squeezed it. "You were great today. You took
on those reporters like it's something you
do all the time."

Ryla turned to him. "Since you told
everyone that we're getting married on
September twenty-second, I think we need
to secure a venue *like yesterday.*"

"I'm already on it," Noel told her. "I gave
them that date because a friend of mine has
some pull over at the Four Seasons in
Houston." He pulled off the highway, and
as they came to a stop he glanced over at
her. "I figured that you'd want to have the
wedding in your hometown instead of
Dallas. Am I correct about that?"

"Absolutely correct. But, Noel, I can't afford the Four Seasons, not even for a
pretend wedding."

He pulled into the parking lot of Bolsa,
switched off the car and turned to her. "I

147

wouldn't dream of having you spend your own money on this wedding. You're doing me a huge favor, and I appreciate it. But I want you to send every bill to me. Okay?"

A wide grin spread across Ryla's face. She leaned over and kissed Noel on the cheek as she said, "I get to have a wedding at the Four Seasons. I've always wanted to get married and have my reception there."

"I remember," Noel said, referring to a comment she'd made to him almost a decade ago. He remembered a lot of things about her.

"It was wonderful, Danetta. He took me to the symphony and then we had dinner in Oak Cliff."

"In Oak Cliff? That's not a very safe neighborhood. Why would Noel take you there?" Danetta asked with concern in her voice.

"His constituents live in Oak Cliff and Noel likes to promote businesses in the area he grew up in. And besides, this restaurant was voted as one of the best spots in Dallas for couples, and I saw for myself why. It was *so* romantic, D."

"If that's the case, Marshall and I need to check this place out."

"You sure do. There's nothing like being

in a romantic atmosphere with your boo by your side."

"What's got you sounding so deliriously happy?"

Gripping the phone tighter, Ryla yelled into the receiver, "Noel made arrangements for us to have the wedding at the Four Seasons."

"That is wonderful, Ryla. Things must be changing between the two of you."

Ryla shrugged, "No change yet. But I can tell that I'm getting to him."

Danetta hesitated for a moment but then slowly said, "I've been thinking."

Ryla knew what was coming and she didn't want to hear it. "No, Danetta, don't start with that do-the-right-thing attitude of yours. You have the man of your dreams. And when you asked for my help, I did everything in my power to help you get him. Now it's my turn."

"I'm not trying to stop you from being with Noel. I just think you should tell him how you really feel. You're just asking for trouble by letting him believe you're on board with his plan, when you know for a fact that you're about to flip the script on him."

Ryla switched the phone from one ear to the other as she sat on the edge of her bed and took her shoes off. "Maybe I shouldn't have called you. It seems like you've been judging every little thing I do from the moment you and Marshall joined your aunt's church."

"I'm sorry you feel that way. Because nothing could be further from the truth. You're my best friend and I just don't want you to get hurt."

Walking barefoot to her closet, Ryla put her after-five pumps back in the shoe box. "Then pray for me, Danetta. You're always talking about how wonderful the women's group at your church is, so why don't you ask them to send a few prayers up for me?" Ryla wasn't sure what she needed to do to help Danetta understand that she loved Noel and didn't want to lose him again.

"I will pray for you, Ryla. But I will also pray that God's will be done in your and Noel's life. Is that all right with you?"

Ryla couldn't think of a single reason why God wouldn't want a man to marry a woman who loved him and he already had a kid by, so she said, "Yes, that's perfect. Now I need to let you go. Jaylen and I will be attending a few summer barbecues and another fundraising dinner with Noel tomorrow."

"He's really putting a lot of effort into

winning this election, huh?" Danetta asked with a hint of admiration in her voice.

"It's important to him. For as long as I've known Noel, he's always talked about helping the people in his community. With a seat in Congress, he'll be able to help thousands instead of the few he's already been helping with the scholarship fund he set up a few years back."

"Noel sounds like a very honorable man," Danetta said.

"He's the real deal, Danetta." Ryla thought back to the days when she and Noel had dated and how she had idolized him.

"Well then, I hope things work out for you, Ryla."

"They will," she said, more determined than ever. "I'll call you next week with more details on the wedding and where you'll need to go to be fitted for your bridesmaid's dress." Ryla and Danetta said their goodbyes.

Ryla hung up and then got ready for bed, all the while imagining how different bedtime would soon be once she was Mrs. Ryla Carter.

CHAPTER 14

"You look happy," Ian said as he walked through the door with a newspaper in hand.

"Do I? Hmmm." Noel leaned back in his chair. He still had a silly grin on his face as he admitted, "I was just thinking about how well Ryla has been handling herself with the rallies, meet and greets, and fundraisers. It's almost as if she was born for political life."

"There's no doubt that she has helped your sorry self." Ian slapped the newspaper down on Noel's desk and pointed to the section that listed poll numbers. "Your numbers are back up. If things continue the way they've been going these last few weeks, you could win this election, my friend."

"If Ryla keeps turning on the charm the way she's been doing, I'll probably win by a landslide," Noel joked.

"Careful, you sound like you're falling," Ian said as he sat on the couch.

Noel moved from behind his desk over to

the chair that was next to his couch. "Watch your mouth with that crazy talk."

"Oh, it's crazy talk, huh?"

"Straitjacket crazy," Noel said as he loosened his tie and began mimicking a man walking around with a straitjacket on. When he sat back down, Noel continued, "Just because I can appreciate the way Ryla handles herself on the campaign trail, it doesn't mean that I've forgotten what she did to me and that she is the reason my poll numbers dropped in the first place."

Ian held up a hand. "Um, she did tell you that it was a bad idea to have Jaylen here for the summer."

Noel waved that notch away. "That was only because she didn't want Jaylen and me to bond. But that's all over now. My baby girl and I are tight." Noel smiled as he thought of Jaylen. "I'm taking her to the Texas Discovery Gardens this weekend to see the free-flying butterflies."

"She will really like that," Ian said, then with a mischievous grin he asked, "So, what do you have planned for Ryla?"

"Oh, don't you worry, I have something special planned for her also. She said she wanted me to date her — well, I just hope she can handle all of what I have in store for her."

"So you're going to do it up for her, huh?"

Noel lifted his collar. "You need to take a few lessons from the master. I know how to keep a woman happy."

A knock on the door interrupted Noel's bragging. "Come in," Noel said.

Cathy walked in. "You told me to remind you about the racket club meeting I set up for you with my sorors."

Noel stood and went back to his desk to check his calendar. "Is that today?"

"It's set for two o'clock this afternoon." Cathy inched closer to Noel's desk as she spoke.

He looked at his watch. "That gives me less than an hour and a half. Is there anything I need to know about this group of women? Any special interest I need to be aware of?"

"Our group is big on literacy, and we host numerous events each year. You should be a guest speaker at a few of those."

"Check," he said while typing that information into the notepad app on his iPad.

"One other thing," Cathy said as she closed the gap between them.

Noel looked up. "What's that?"

"They don't like for their guest to be late or look unkempt." She grabbed hold of his tie and slowly tightened it back around his neck. When she was finished with the tie, she straightened his collar and smoothed out his shirt. She licked her lips as she looked back up at him. There was hardly any daylight between them as she said, "I've already put in a good word for you, so you should do fine."

It wasn't her words, it was the way she said them that made Noel think that something other than business was going on, and he didn't want any part of it. He was just about to step away from Cathy when his door slammed. Noel jumped and glanced toward the door. There Ryla stood, breathing fire out her nose.

Ian jumped up. "Is anything wrong, Ryla? Can I help you with something?"

Noel wanted to advise Ian to just step out of the way. Ryla was about to blow and nothing either of them said was going to stop it.

"I think I just figured out that I wasn't crazy after all," Ryla said as her eyes darted from Cathy to Noel.

Noel lifted hands in protest. "Ryla, this is not at all what it looks like. Cathy was just straightening my tie because I have to be at a meeting in a little while."

"Oh, so are my eyes playing tricks on me again? Is that what's going on, Noel? Or did

I just catch you cuddling up with —" she pointed at Cathy "— this man-stealing woman again?"

"Again?" Cathy said, with confusion written on her face.

Ryla turned on her. "I saw you kiss Noel in the locker room when we were in college. I've known for a very long time that you want to be with him."

"Look, Ryla . . ." Cathy began.

"Don't you *look, Ryla* me." Ryla held out her ring finger, prominently displaying her engagement ring. "Does this ring on my finger mean nothing to you? How dare you try to steal him away from me again."

"Baby, calm down," Noel said as he watched Ryla fume. He had never seen her this angry. And now he wondered if there might be some deeper issue Ryla was dealing with that would cause her to respond in this manner when he hadn't done anything.

She turned on him. "And don't you dare call me baby. You're just as bad as she is. I told you to fire her, but you refused." Tears stung Ryla's face as she twisted the gorgeous ring off her finger. "Well, you can forget about our little engagement, because I wouldn't marry you if we had three kids out of wedlock." She threw the ring at him and ran out of the building.

Noel didn't know what to do. He was caught in the midst of a dilemma, wanting to run after Ryla to put that ring back on her finger, but not understanding why, since he had no interest in marrying her in the first place. He picked up the ring off the floor and then plopped down in his chair.

"I — I'm sorry about this," Cathy said as she rushed out of the room.

Ian got up and walked toward the door. "I don't think I'll be needing those lessons," he said with a smirk on his face.

Noel shook his head. "Kick a brother while he's down, huh? I see how you are."

"The way I see it, you're not down or out. There's only one reason why a woman would be that angry at a man." With his hand on the doorknob, Ian added, "Think about it, and then go get your woman back."

Yawning and stretching in bed, Ryla glanced at her ring finger, and the emptiness of it brought tears to her eyes again. Noel must think her a fool . . . throwing a fake engagement ring at him and refusing to marry him when he'd never wanted to marry her in the first place.

So much for being sweet and loving, as Danetta had advised. When she'd walked into Noel's office and seen Cathy acting as if she was Noel's office woman, she'd lost her cool. That woman had been after her man for ten years now — when would she finally give up? Ryla turned over in bed as she came to the conclusion that she might be the one who needed to give up.

Her stomach growled as she inhaled the aromas coming from the kitchen. She hadn't felt like eating last night. Aunt Shelly had practically begged her to eat. She'd even gone so far as to fix peach cobbler, Ryla's favorite dessert. But her heart wouldn't let her eat a thing. Even now, with the aroma of bacon and sausage tickling her nose, Ryla couldn't find the strength to climb out of bed.

Why had she agreed to Noel's crazy idea in the first place? *Because I planned to trick him into marrying me,* she reminded herself. But Ryla could never marry a cheater, no matter how much her heart cried out for him. *I survived this once, I'll survive it again.* She punched her pillow and pulled the covers over her head. Ryla wanted to sleep the day away, but Jaylen would never let that happen. She was supposed to be going to the Texas Discovery Gardens with her and Noel today to take the butterfly tour. At noon hundreds of tropical butterflies were released into the Rosine Smith Sammons

158

Butterfly House and Insectarium.

Jaylen was excited because she imagined the sight of hundreds of butterflies flying around with their multicolored wings would be beautiful. Ryla prayed that Noel would show up to take Jaylen to that butterfly house. But her own experience with daddies' not showing up once they were no longer in a relationship with the mother was enough to make her want to keep Jaylen's expectations low.

After her father had left her mother, he rarely ever kept his word about picking her up. There was always something more important that came up. When he had more children, it seemed as though Ryla had been pushed further out of his life, because by then her visits had been totally cut off.

Sinking deeper into her pillow-top mattress, Ryla wiped tears from her eyes. She wasn't looking forward to saying, "Your father is a very busy man. Something really important must have come up to keep him from picking you up today," as her mother used to say to her all the time. This was the very thing that she wanted to spare Jaylen.

Just as she was contemplating getting out of bed to search for the address of the Texas Discovery Gardens in case she would have to take Jaylen herself, the door to her bedroom burst open.

Jaylen ran in and jumped on her bed. "Mommy, Mommy, wake up. We have to get ready so we can go see the butterflies."

She looked at her watch. It was nine-thirty in the morning. Noel had said the butterflies were released at noon. Lifting up, Ryla said, "Okay baby, let me call your dad. He may have a rally to attend today. So I might be taking you to see the butterflies myself."

"What are you talking about, Mommy?" Jaylen giggled. "Daddy's downstairs fixing breakfast."

She flipped the covers off. "He's where?"

"Downstairs. He wants to fix us breakfast before we leave."

Grabbing a comb, Ryla headed for the bathroom. "Go tell your father that I'll be down there in a minute."

She jumped in the shower, brushed her teeth, then took off her bonnet and un-wrapped her hair in record time. Back in her bedroom, she fumbled around her closet trying to figure out what she should wear. Technically, she should still be angry with him about fooling around with Cathy while supposedly being engaged to her. But just the fact that he had shown up for Jaylen made her want to take Danetta's advice again. She would watch her attitude but remain casual. Throwing on a pair of white linen Bermuda shorts and a pink fitted tank top, Ryla slipped on her sandals and headed downstairs.

Jaylen and Aunt Shelly were seated at the table while Noel passed several plates over to them, filled with French toast, bacon, sausage and eggs.

"Orange juice coming up," Noel said as he headed back to the kitchen counter. As he began pouring the juice in the cups, he looked up and smiled. "Hey, sleepyhead."

What was she supposed to say to that? He was acting as if nothing happened between them yesterday. She reminded herself that she was grateful that he bothered to show up for his daughter and said, "Hey."

"Grab a seat — breakfast is still hot," Noel told her while placing the syrup on the table.

"And good," Aunt Shelly said, busy chewing and cutting up her French toast.

Noel pulled a chair out for her. "I know you like French toast, because you were making it that day I visited your house."

She sat down and filled her plate without saying anything. Ryla figured the less she said, the better, especially because her feelings were conflicted.

"I wish I could see all those butterflies." Aunt Shelly shook her head. "I can't believe that I've lived in Dallas all my life and I've never seen the release of those butterflies."

"Come with us, Auntie Shelly," Jaylen said to her great-aunt and then asked Noel, "She can come with us, can't she, Daddy?"

"Of course," Noel said as he sat down next to Ryla. "Your mom can come, too, if she wants."

No, he didn't. Nice was one thing, but she wasn't about to let him act as if he was some rolling stone, hanging his hat here today and at Cathy's house the next. She held up her ring finger and shook it in his face. "Have you forgotten?"

Noel stood up and dug in his jean pocket. "I found your ring. We can get it re-sized if you think it might slip off again."

He looked so innocent, so serious and so cute as he gently placed the beautiful three-carat diamond ring back in her hand. She wanted so badly to put that ring back on her finger, but she would never wear a cheater's ring. He'd fooled her once about Cathy, but she knew she wasn't crazy now. Something was going on, and Noel needed to explain himself. Abruptly, she put down her fork and stood. "Can I speak to you in the family room, please?" she pointedly said to Noel.

Kissing Jaylen on the top of the head,

Noel stepped away from the table and followed Ryla. "I'll be right back, baby girl."

"Okay, Daddy, just don't forget to put Mommy's ring back on her finger. She was pretty sad about losing it," Jaylen innocently said, and then turned back to her food as if she hadn't just told on her mom.

Noel was pretending that everything was fine between them, so Ryla did her best to pretend that she wasn't completely embarrassed by Jaylen's comment. When Ryla was a kid, her mother always told her that she shouldn't tell outsiders anything that went on inside their house. Ryla would now have to have that conversation with her own child. Noel might be Jaylen's father, but as of right now, Ryla wasn't sure if she wanted to have anything to do with him.

Once in the family room, Ryla crossed her arms. "What are you trying to pull? Didn't you get the memo that I don't want to be engaged to you anymore when I threw the ring at your head?"

"Baby, look . . ." Noel began.

Ryla wagged a finger at him. "Watch yourself. I don't allow cheaters to call me that."

He stepped closer to her, took her hand in his and looked her in the eye as he slid the ring back on her finger. "Then we don't

163

have a problem, because I've never cheated on you."

CHAPTER 15

Noel couldn't explain the feeling of joy he experienced as he toured the butterfly house with Jaylen and Ryla. Aunt Shelly had changed her mind right before they left the house. Noel suspected that she wanted him to be able to spend time along with his family. Whoa . . . Where did that thought come from? Yes, Jaylen was his daughter, but Ryla was not part of his family and it would do him well to remember that in the weeks to come.

But Noel was having a hard time taking his own advice as he and Ryla walked hand in hand through the butterfly house, watching butterflies dance around them.

"Daddy, look, the butterflies got me!" Jaylen called out, as several butterflies nested in her head.

"Not as long as your daddy is here." Noel stood in a Captain America stance and sang, "Daddy, to the rescue." He made as if he was diving toward Jaylen. Then with care, he freed her hair of all the butterflies.

Jaylen and Ryla giggled at his antics. Then as Noel turned toward Ryla, butterflies dancing in her hair also, he leaned into Jaylen and said, "Captain Daddy has to save Mommy now." She looked so beautiful that he just had to touch her.

"What? I don't have any butterflies on me," Ryla said.

Noel kept walking toward her. Ryla had gotten most of the butterflies off her, but one still hung on, giving him an excuse to run his hand through her hair. "Stand still," he said, as he slowly pulled his hands through her hair, took the butterfly out and showed it to Ryla. "See, Captain Daddy can save you, too," he told her with hunger in his eyes. When she didn't move away from him, but rather tilted her head backward, staring at him, he lost himself in her penetrating brown eyes. Noel prayed that she wanted to be kissed, because he couldn't help but lower his head and devour her mouth.

"Daddy's kissing Mommy, Daddy's kissing Mommy," Jaylen sang.

Backing away from Ryla as he came to his senses, Noel grinned and told Jaylen, "I had to make her feel better about being attacked by those swarms of butterflies."

"Then I need a kiss, too."

"Okay, baby girl, you got it." Noel picked his daughter up, swung her around and then planted wet kisses on her forehead and both her cheeks.

"Stop, Daddy. You didn't give Mommy that many kisses."

"Little girls need more kisses than big girls after being attacked by butterflies." Noel kept kissing his daughter on each cheek, again and again.

"Mommy, make Daddy stop. Little girls don't need these many kisses."

He put Jaylen down. As the three of them walked out of the butterfly house, he told her, "I'm just making up for lost time, Jaylen. Sorry if I gave you too many kisses." A bit of sadness touched Noel's eyes as he thought of all the time he missed out on giving kisses and hugs to his daughter. He sighed as he tried, with everything in him, not to go back to his place of anger.

When they got in the car and Noel was driving them back home, he glanced in the back and noticed that Jaylen had fallen asleep. He then directed his attention to Ryla.

"I won't claim to understand this fixation you have with cheating men, and why you keep trying to put me in that category, but, Ryla, I swear to you . . . I'm not interested in Cathy."

"You might not be interested in Cathy, but she is interested in you, Noel. The sooner you face that, the better it will be for all of us."

As Noel pulled up to a stoplight and glanced over at Ryla, he saw fear in her eyes and realized that she was dealing with him from a place of pain. Someone had hurt her, and since he always thought that he was her first love, Noel was once again clueless in trying to understand Ryla's pain.

Noel's eyes darted to the backseat again. His little girl was still sleeping soundly. He turned back to Ryla and asked, "Who hurt you, Ryla?" He held up a hand, stopping her before she had the chance to respond. "I know you want to blame your issues on me, but I didn't cheat on you. You left me before discovering or even seeking out the truth, so somebody must have hurt you before we ever met."

She turned to the window and stared out into the sky.

"I can't help you if you don't talk to me about this."

She turned back to him and held up her left hand. "I took your ring back, so I must believe you. I just think that women like Cathy O'Dell have been breaking up marriages since the beginning of time, and if you don't watch it, you're going to lose your family, too."

He noticed that she hadn't answered his question about who hurt her, but instead warned him about losing his family. That comment brought him back to when they were in the butterfly house, and thoughts of them being a family sent shivers down his spine. Noel wanted to correct Ryla, but knowing that she was dealing with heavier matters, he shook it off and directed the conversation to their upcoming wedding. "We have an appointment to meet with the hostess at the Four Seasons on Tuesday. I can fly us down and fly back that afternoon. Will that work for you?"

"I could call my mother and have her meet us there. She's been itching to help me with the wedding plans. And since we'll be getting married in Houston, she'll be able to take care of things for me while we're campaigning in Dallas."

There was no reason for him to be excited over Ryla agreeing to marry him again, especially since he had asked her to jilt him at the altar . . . but he was.

The Four Seasons was absolutely spectacular, and Ryla couldn't believe that Noel had remembered where she wanted to have her wedding reception, based on a conversation they had so long ago. "Can you believe how beautiful this place is?" Ryla said to her mother as they toured the grounds of the hotel. Jaylen had stayed in Dallas with Aunt Shelly so that she would be able to give her full attention to the planning of this wedding.

Looking around in wonder, Juanita said, "You always did have expensive taste."

"Tell me about it," Noel joked. "I was only twenty-one when she told me about this place. I made up my mind back then to make her dream come true, even though at the time I knew nothing about this place."

Juanita patted him on the shoulder. "Well, thank God that you have the money to make my daughter's dreams come true."

"Mother," Ryla said, as she blushed from embarrassment.

"It's okay, baby." Noel grabbed Ryla, twirled her around and wrapped his arms around her as he kissed her neck. "I'm glad that I could do this for you."

Noel was playing the loving fiancé to the hilt. When she agreed to fake marry him, Noel had strongly expressed that no one was to know that their engagement wasn't the real thing. But now Noel was playing too much into her emotions, and she didn't like that. Pulling herself out of his arms, Ryla turned to the wedding coordinator and asked, "Can we see the ballroom?"

"Right this way," Melinda, their hired wedding planner, cheerfully said.

When they entered the ballroom, Ryla was immediately swept away as she pictured herself and Noel dancing below the hand-blown Venetian-glass chandelier. The entire room was gorgeous, filled with beautiful bouquets in clear glass vases that stood five feet tall. "Now, this is breathtaking."

Melinda jotted something down on her iPad. She then gave them a tour of the room. When she was finished, she told them, "The Four Seasons offers white and sand-colored linen for your banquet. If you're interested in another color, that would need to be special ordered."

"The sand-colored linen works for me," Ryla said, then she pointed at the standing flower bouquets. "I also like the way you have these flowers around the room. Is this standard?"

Melinda quickly typed Ryla's comments and then said, "No, the flowers are not standard, but if you like this design, I can definitely make it happen."

Noel nodded. "We like."

Next, Melinda showed them the grand staircase, where the bridal party would be able to take pictures. Ryla was handed pamphlets on flower arrangements, catering, entertainment, cakes and much more. She was beginning to feel a bit overwhelmed. And then Melinda asked if they would be staying overnight.

Noel quickly answered. "We'll stay two nights after the wedding." He put his arm around Ryla and added, "I'll need to get back on the campaign trail after that. So, the missus and I will have to plan a full honeymoon after the election."

Ryla looked at Noel as if he had lost his mind with all this after-the-wedding talk, but then she wondered if he knew her intentions and was just trying to smoke her out. Or maybe he'd changed his mind about her leaving him at the altar and now wanted to get married just as much as she did.

"So, would you like to pick a hotel suite or check out the place where we'll hold the wedding ceremony?" Melinda asked.

"I don't know about Ryla, but I'd like to

pick our honeymoon suite and then we can check out the ceremonial spot afterward."

Juanita nudged her daughter. "He's anxious, isn't he?"

"Please stop embarrassing me," Ryla whispered to her mother.

"Ah, girl, hush, I was young once, too, you know." Juanita smacked Ryla's bottom. "Now let's go see the suite you'll be staying in for your honeymoon."

"Which rooms do you have available?" Noel asked Melinda as they headed toward the elevator.

"We have several executive suites available for the weekend of your wedding. But the Governor's Suite and the Presidential Suite, which are both located on our top floor, are also available."

They stepped into the elevator. Noel said, "I've never wanted to be a governor, so why don't we go ahead and check out the Presidential Suite?"

Melinda took them to the twentieth floor and let them out in front of the spacious nineteen-hundred-square-foot suite fit for a king.

While Ryla's mother stood in the living area of the suite, oohing and aahing, Ryla grabbed Noel's arm and pulled him into the bedroom. "Can I speak with you for a moment?"

"Sure, baby, what's up?"

Ryla planted her hands on her hips as she stood at front him. "What is this all about?"

He scrunched his eyebrows. "I'm not following."

"Why in the world did you ask for the Presidential Suite? Do you know how much this room costs?"

He sauntered over to her, bent down and nibbled on her lip. "So you don't want to spend the weekend in this luxurious space with me?"

Her hands went to his chest and she pushed him away. "Have you forgotten that I'm supposed to leave you at the altar?" she whispered while watching the door to make sure her mother wasn't walking into the bedroom.

"Look, Ryla, this whole Four Seasons thing is not just your dream." He sat down on the four-poster king-size bed. "Ever since you told me about this place, I have been dreaming of the day I would marry you here."

"But you don't want me to marry you," Ryla reminded him.

"That's no reason not to enjoy the journey." He winked and then pulled her so close that she was standing between his legs.

"You could have your bags brought up here earlier in the day, so when you leave me at the altar, you can just run up here. We could order massages or something and relax."

No, he wasn't coming on to her . . . trying to sleep with her even though he didn't want to go all the way and marry her. Now she didn't feel so bad about tricking him into marrying her. Matter of fact, she would take that massage.

"Melinda," Ryla called out.

When Melinda came into the bedroom, Ryla looked directly at Noel and, calling his bluff, she said, "We'll take this suite and we'd like couple's massages also."

Melinda jotted that information down. "Anything else?"

"Yes, I'd like to see the area for the wedding ceremony," Ryla said as she pulled away from Noel.

"Where are you going? I thought you brought me into this room so we could try out the bed," Noel said as he tried to pull her back.

"I'm not going to try out that bed until my wedding day, thank you very much," she told him and meant every word. She was done sleeping with Noel Carter without the commitment of marriage.

Melinda took them all back down to the

lobby. As they were headed outdoors, Ryla heard her mother yell, "Ryan, what in the world took you so long?"

No. No, it can't be, Ryla thought as she whirled around and came face-to-face with her absentee father.

"What are you doing here?" Ryla asked as Ryan attempted to hug her.

"Your mother told me that I needed to give away the bride." He kissed her on the cheek. "I'm so happy for you, Ryla."

Ryan then turned to Noel and stuck out his hand. "I'm Ryla's father, Ryan Evans."

Noel took his hand. "Nice to meet you, sir. I'm Noel."

"Boy, I know who you are. I'm just glad to see that my daughter has done so well for herself." Ryan then turned his attention to Melinda. He slowly took the woman's hand and kissed it. "And who is this lovely lady?"

Ryla absolutely could not believe what was happening right in front of her face. She hadn't been in her father's presence for more than a minute and he was already flirting with some woman who wasn't his wife. Ryla felt compelled to remind him that he was a thrice-married man.

She cleared her throat. "I doubt if your third wife would appreciate you checking out my wedding coordinator, Dad."

He looked at her nonchalantly and said, "Sylvia and I are separated."

Ryla couldn't stand Sylvia. In the eleven years she'd been married to her father, the woman had never made an effort to get to know her. But even though she couldn't stand Sylvia, Ryla knew with everything in her that the separation was due to her father's wandering eyes. It wasn't enough that he destroyed her mother with his cheating ways — he also had to destroy the relationship that he was supposed to have with his daughter. Ryan Evans thought the fact that he was tall, handsome and made a decent living meant he could do whatever he wanted to these unsuspecting women, and that made her sick.

At that moment, Ryla realized that if she never in her life saw her father again, that would be just fine with her. She pointed toward the exit and screamed, "Get out! I don't want you here."

Ryan dropped Melinda's hand and turned toward his daughter. "What did you say?"

"You heard me." Ryla's voice was still blaring. "You never spent any time with me when I was younger . . . too busy out chasing women to notice that I needed a father in my life. But guess what? I don't need you now. And I don't want you here."

Noel pulled Ryla close to him as the guests in the lobby stopped and stared. "Baby, calm down."

"No!" she continued to scream. "Get him out of here. I don't want him anywhere near me."

Juanita put her hand on Ryla's back and began to rub circles. "I'm sorry, Ryla. I didn't know you would be this upset by seeing your father or I never would have asked him to walk you down the aisle."

Ryan's eyes were moist as he told her, "I know I didn't spend enough time with you while you were growing up. But that doesn't mean I don't love you."

She laughed at him. "I'm not that eight-year-old girl, crying for my daddy anymore. I don't need you, so just go."

While Noel held Ryla close to him and Juanita rubbed her back, Ryan walked over and placed a kiss on his daughter's forehead. "I'm sorry I wasn't there, sweetheart. But I'd like to be here for you now if you'll let me."

CHAPTER 16

As Noel watched Ryla turn into a bridezilla over her father offering to walk her down the aisle, everything clicked into place. Ryan Evans, Mr. Three Wives and working on number four, was the main reason for her heartache. Ryla didn't trust all men because of one man, this man, standing before them, claiming that he was now ready to be a father.

"My mother can walk me down the aisle," Ryla said venomously. "You don't deserve that honor."

"I paid my child support," Ryan said, clearly taking offense at Ryla's remarks.

Her eyes pleaded with Noel as she turned to him. "Get me out of here. I can't be in the same space with this man."

Struck by the pain he saw in her eyes, Noel immediately went into protector mode. On the court he was known for dribbling and shooting, but he could block and guard just as well. Hugging Ryla tightly to him, Noel shuffled her out the door and toward the area where the wedding ceremony would take place.

He sat her down in one of the lawn chairs and bent down in front of her. "Are you okay?"

In response, Ryla threw her arms around Noel's neck and laid her head on his shoulder as she shook from the tears. "Just keep him away from me."

Noel held her tight. "Ah, baby, don't cry. He just wants to take part in our wedding."

She shook her head. "I don't want him anywhere near me. Not even for this wedding."

What did she mean by *this wedding*? Was Ryla diminishing the importance of what they were doing, just because he refused to go all the way into a marriage of convenience? He leaned back on his heels and lifted her chin with his index finger. "Ryla, look around — there is nothing second-rate about what we are doing. And I plan to enjoy every moment of it, all the way up to the moment you break my heart again."

She wiped the tears from her face. "But I don't have to break your heart, Noel. And you don't have to break mine. We could —"

"Okay, Ryla, I took care of everything.

Your father is gone and he won't bother you until after the wedding," Juanita said as she joined them.

Noel jumped up. He knew what Ryla was about to ask him, and if Juanita had waited five more minutes to join them, Ryla probably would have talked him into it. What was going on here? Had he been enjoying himself so much that he'd forgotten who Ryla was and what she had done? Not to mention the fact that Ryla's view of men was damaged by what her father had done to her. And Noel refused to pay for another man's mistake.

Ryla and Juanita walked off with Melinda, viewing the ceremonial area as Noel tried to regain his senses. His cell phone rang. Noel pulled the phone off the holder on his belt, checked the caller ID and then answered, grateful for the distraction. "Ian, my man, what can I do for you?"

"We have a problem, buddy. Where are you?"

"I'm in Houston with Ryla. We're taking care of the final details for the wedding."

"This is not good," Ian said.

"My schedule was clear," Noel reminded him. "I don't have another event until tomorrow afternoon."

"Dan Bridges was just at a televised event

where he politely told everyone that with known womanizing, sexual abuse charges won't be too far behind, referring to you, of course."

Noel held up a hand. "Now, hold on, I've never sexually harassed a woman in my life." He shrugged with a confident swagger. "Never had to."

"It's comments like that that are going to lose this election for you. Because Dan is also telling anyone who'll listen that you are now more concerned about your love life than the business of governing."

"Dan says something negative about me every day of the week. He's fighting hard to win this election, just as I am. So, for you to be so worried about something Dan said, it tells me one thing — my poll numbers must have dropped again."

"Actually, your poll numbers are holding steady. And I think Ryla has a lot to do with that. With a pretty girl like Ryla on your arm, nobody believes that you have your mind on anyone else."

"Then we don't have a problem," Noel said, watching Ryla beam as she spoke with Melinda and her mom. He could tell that she had pushed those bad thoughts of her dad away and was once again dazzled by the thought of having her dream wedding.

"Our problem is this ridiculous runaway-bride idea of yours. I told you that a marriage of convenience would help your political career flourish. But if Ryla runs off, then the voters might believe what Dan said about you being too busy chasing skirts to put in the work that will benefit Texas."

"That's ludicrous!" Noel thundered.

"Ludicrous or not, if enough voters believe it, you'll be toast, my friend."

"Why do you always call me 'my friend' when you say the unfriendliest things to me?"

"You want some sugar, go kiss Ryla. My job is to tell you the truth and help you figure out a way around it," Ian said.

"Well, it sounds like we need to figure something out on this one, and fast." Noel looked at his watch. "I chartered a plane, so I can be back in Dallas in about two hours." He hung up and returned to Ryla, placing his hand on her lower back and brushing a kiss across her lips.

"Is everything okay?" she asked with concern in her voice.

"That was Ian. We need to put out a fire, so I have to head back to Dallas."

She held up the pamphlets for the caterer, entertainment, flowers and so on. "I can't leave right now. I still have a ton of decisions to make."

"Do you mind if I head back today? I'll send the airplane back for you in the morning?"

"What are we going to do with Jaylen if I spend the night here?" Ryla worried.

"I'll pick Jaylen up from your aunt's house. She can spend the night with me."

"Don't fill her up on ice cream." Ryla wagged her pointer finger in his face. "Make her eat a balanced dinner."

"Hey, she eats healthy when she's with me." Noel objected to the chastisement.

"You always give in to her, and you know that I'm right."

"You two sound like you've been co-parenting for years," Juanita broke in. "Let him go spoil his daughter so we can get back to planning this fabulous wedding."

Noel kissed Juanita on the cheek. "Thanks, Mama Evans."

"Don't encourage him, Mama."

Noel wrapped his arms around Ryla. "I'll take you to dinner tomorrow night." He then pulled her closer and whispered in her ear, "Or I could stop by and make breakfast for you again."

She pushed him away. "Get out of here. I have a lot of planning to do."

■ ■ ■ ■

Ryla and her mother stayed at the Four
Seasons until they had the food, flowers,
entertainment and invitations picked out.
She was tired by the time she left, but since
she only had one night in Houston, she met
up with Danetta and Surry at Casa de
Novia Bridal Couture. The three women
viewed gowns by designers such as Vera
Wang, Oscar de la Renta and several other
couturiers. Ryla didn't have much time for
second-guessing, so before they left she
decided on a simple-cut, full-length gown
by Junko Yoshioka. They even found rose-
colored bridesmaid dresses that were perfect
for Danetta and Surry.

"Thanks for not making us wear ugly
dresses," Surry said as they sat down to a
late-night dinner at Mama's Café.

"I wouldn't dream of putting you or
Danetta in anything but the most glamor-
ous dress we can afford. And since Noel is
paying for everything . . . we can afford
those gorgeous gowns." Ryla giggled as she
took a bite of her turkey sandwich.

"That's the first time you've mentioned
Noel's name since we met up with you.
What gives?" Danetta asked.

"I don't know." Ryla shrugged. "Noel told me that I should take time to enjoy every moment of our engagement, because this is something that we both dreamed about doing. But I think seeing my father today kind of startled me."

"Why would seeing your father while planning your wedding startle you?" Surry asked.

"He's just such a cheater. . . . The man is separated from his third wife and on the prowl for wife number four." Ryla shook her head. "Anyway, after seeing him I started thinking that maybe I should just do what Noel wants. Enjoy my engagement and then run for my life before I say 'I do.' "

Danetta and Surry sat stunned in silence.

"Don't everyone speak at once," Ryla said as her friends kept looking at her as if they'd been mummified.

"We both know that I'm not going to talk you out of doing the right thing," Danetta said.

Surry elbowed Danetta. "Well, if she won't, then I will. It is obvious to me that this man cares for you. Why else would he be doing everything he's done concerning this wedding?"

Stirring her iced tea with a straw, Ryla said, "That's my fear . . . What if I force him to marry me and then he becomes so angry that he starts cheating on me out of spite? I wouldn't be able to deal with that."

"What I don't understand is why you automatically assume every man is a cheater."

"Oh, that's right, you've never met my father," Ryla deadpanned.

Danetta sighed. "I hate that your father treated your mother so poorly and that he allowed his cheating to affect his relationship with you, but you need to forgive that man and let it go."

"Right after he begs for my forgiveness, I might think about it."

"I'm with Ryla on this one," Surry said. "Some people do so much dirt that they'll need to beg until Jesus comes back before forgiveness comes their way."

"Don't encourage her, Surry. Ryla needs to get past this thing with her father if she is ever going to have a loving and trusting relationship with any man."

"All right, Dr. Danetta. Thank you for diagnosing my problem, and I will take it into consideration. But right now all I can think about is Noel and Jaylen," Ryla said.

"How is Jaylen doing?" Surry asked as she put a forkful of her grilled-chicken salad into her mouth.

"She loves Dallas. I don't know how I'm going to get her to come back home when the summer is over."

"If you marry Noel, you wouldn't have to come back home," Surry reminded her.

"Why don't you have a talk with Noel? Check to see where his head is at right now. You never know — the two of you might want the same thing," Danetta encouraged.

"You might be right, Danetta. Before I make a final decision involving Jaylen, I'm going to talk to Noel about what I want for us, and the fear I have about marrying a man like my father."

Danetta patted Ryla's hand, "You're making the right decision."

Ryla was so confused right now that she didn't know what decision to make. If she married Noel, she would forever be on edge, wondering if he was going to leave her for someone else. If she walked away, she would destroy her little girl. Noel had worried about how their scheme would affect Jaylen, but Ryla hadn't worried at all. Because all the while she had been scheming on him: planning to say "I do" even though he didn't want her to. But now that she was considering walking away, she wished she had listened to his concerns about how this would affect Jaylen in the long run, after all.

CHAPTER 17

Four Weeks Later

Ryla stood in the mirror looking back at her reflection. She was in a beautiful floor-length, cream-colored wedding gown that made her look more elegant than the Duchess of Cambridge had on her wedding day. As a matter of fact, with the way Noel had treated her over the past few weeks of their engagement, she felt as if she were Kate Middleton marrying her prince.

Noel had kept his word by taking her out and making her feel special every time he had the opportunity. She had grown so comfortable with him that she'd begun to believe that this was all real. But as she stood at the mirror looking at a reflection of herself, she realized that these past weeks with Noel had only been an illusion and she was playing a dangerous game of deception.

Ryla should have been the happiest woman at the Four Seasons, but she felt as if she was being tossed by winds and waves that she couldn't control. "Will you look at the mess you've gotten yourself in," she said to her reflection. "Jaylen wants you to marry her father, but Noel wants you to run." She finally asked herself, "What do you want?"

No answer came from the mirror, but as she continued to stare at herself she remembered that odd man she'd seen at the mall who had shown her a reflection of herself after having her read the front of his little black book, which asked, "Who did Jesus die for?"

She had forgotten about that strange man, so why that incident would cross her mind on her wedding day, of all days, was beyond her understanding. She turned away from the mirror as her makeup artist and hairstylist came through the door to begin fussing over her.

Her mother walked in a few minutes later, stopped in front of her and burst into tears. "You look so beautiful." She took Ryla's arm, lifted it and twirled her around. "You are always stylish, but this gown is so elegant."

Hugging her mother, Ryla said, "Thank you for saying that, and thank you for being here for me today."

"About that, honey." Juanita hesitated.

"What's wrong, Mom?"

"Well, honey, I don't want you to get mad and make a scene on your wedding day, but your daddy is waiting outside the door to speak with you."

Ryla started shaking her head. "What? No. Why would you let him in here?"

"I can't stop him from coming into the hotel, Ryla," Juanita pleaded.

"I don't want to see him."

Juanita asked everyone to leave the room and then she grabbed hold of her daughter's arm and sat her down on a beige sofa nearby. "It's your wedding day and I'm so proud of you, so I don't want to argue. But, Ryla Evans, you have got to let go of the hatred you have for your father."

"I don't hate him," she said.

"You're stubborn, Ryla — you get that from me. I know it and I'm not proud of it." Juanita's eyes took on a sorrowful expression as she said, "I spent years being angry with my sister over an argument we had. I wouldn't speak to her or go and visit. When she got sick last year and I had to visit her in the hospital, it nearly killed me. Don't be like me, Ryla. Don't waste years of your life holding a grudge. Live and love now, before it's too late."

Ryla remembered how torn her mother

had been when Aunt Shelly had had surgery last year. She'd practically moved herself to Dallas trying to make up for the years of absence and foolishness. At that moment, Ryla realized that if something bad happened to her father, she would indeed regret not allowing him to be a part of her life. "Tell him to come in."

Juanita hopped up. "Okay, honey. I'll be right back."

As Ryla watched her father walk into her dressing room, her mind's eye was remembering another day. He was younger, but still just as handsome, as he walked out of their house, holding a suitcase and promising to call her.

She stood up, smoothed out her dress and told him, "You missed out on some really good years of my life."

He stood before her humbled as he sighed and nodded.

"In high school I was captain of the cheerleading squad, but you never came to one game. I was crowned homecoming queen in college. . . . You weren't there that day, either. So, I guess I just don't understand why it's so important for you to be here now."

"I should have been there at all of those other events."

"You missed the birth of your granddaughter also," Ryla reminded him.

He lowered his head. After a moment, he looked at her and said, "I have no excuses, sweetie. I got lost in myself. Thinking that I only needed to be concerned about my own happiness, but in the end I became the most miserable of all." He broke down and cried in front of her.

Ryla's heart broke at the sight of her father's tears. Her issues with him may have cost her years away from Noel, but she still didn't want this. Ryla reached up and wiped the tears from his face.

He grabbed her hand. "Please don't let me miss this occasion. If you never want to see me again after today, I'll understand. But let me walk my little girl down the aisle, please."

All Ryla had ever wanted was a relationship with her dad. And as he stood before her, pleading to take part in her wedding, all the years of sitting on the window seat waiting for him to pick her up seemed to fade away. She wrapped her arms around her dad and blubbered, "Thanks for being here."

Jaylen gracefully walked down the aisle, tossing roses petals with every step she took.

The bridesmaids and groomsmen were standing next to Noel as he beamed over his little girl and how sweet she was. To this day, Noel still couldn't believe his good fortune in having a child as precious as Jaylen. He'd take five more just like her, with a boy tossed in for good measure.

Jaylen made it down the aisle, stood next to him and asked loud enough for the first three rows of guests to hear, "Did I do a good job, Daddy?"

Noel bent down and whispered in her ear, "You did a perfect job, baby girl."

Jaylen beamed and Noel's heart expanded in his chest. He'd only known his little girl for a short time, but already he couldn't imagine a day without her. When this was all over between him and Ryla, Noel didn't know how he would go back to only weekend visits.

As the "Bridal Chorus" began to play, Noel raised his head to look down the aisle and caught the loveliest vision in white that he'd ever seen. Ryla's dress was silky and dangled all the way to the floor. She held on to her father's arm as she walked down the aisle, looking nervous and unsure of herself. Noel found himself drifting back to the days when their love was so real and all he wanted to do was graduate from college, and start his basketball career so he'd be earning enough to take care of a wife and kids. How he wished that Ryla had waited for him. Noel wished with everything in him that she hadn't run away from him and had told him about their child. He wished the two of them had been together all these years and that there had been no other women. But just wishing wouldn't make it so.

Ryla was who she was, and he doubted that he would ever be able to change her. Sometimes he even wondered if Ryla truly knew just how much she'd cost him by leaving as she did. Drinking and gambling had never been his style, but once Ryla left, he seemed to need a drink just to make it through the day. The gambling had been his means of recreation since he had nothing better to do . . . and the women? He kept trying to replace Ryla. But nothing he did took Ryla out of his heart, so he did more and more of it. Until he became a weekly tabloid favorite.

He couldn't go back down that road again, not even to win this election. Ian had already warned him that when Ryla walked out on him today, he could kiss his political career goodbye. Noel was used to transition and figuring out new dreams when old ones

195

suddenly were no longer available to him. He'd do the same thing if he lost this election. He could survive that. But Noel wasn't so sure he could survive Ryla walking out on him again. Not in a million years.

Ryla's father handed her off to him. Noel grabbed her hand and pulled her close to him. Noel wanted to lean over and whisper in her ear, "Marry me for real." But he kept his mouth shut, even though he knew that his heart would surely break the moment Ryla walked out on him. But better she do it now, rather than later.

The preacher cleared his throat as they stood before him. When he opened his mouth he read from the book of Genesis and quoted Proverbs, "Who findeth a wife findeth a good thing and obtains favor from the Lord."

The preacher went on to encourage them about the benefits of marriage. He then turned to the guests and asked, "Is there anyone here who knows of a reason these two should not be joined together?"

Noel wanted to raise his hands. Because the reason they *should* be joined together was standing next to them holding a basket of rose petals. As much as Noel wanted to make this thing between himself and Ryla real, he knew he had to trust her beyond any doubts. No marriage could work without trust.

No one spoke out against Ryla or Noel, so the preacher continued. He turned to Noel and said, "Repeat after me."

Noel held on to Ryla's hand, looked her in the eye and waited for the opportunity to repeat his vows.

The preacher stated the first line of the vows, and then Noel said, "I, Noel Carter, take you, Ryla Evans, to be my wedded wife." With those first words, Noel felt as if his heart was about to explode. He wanted to bend down, grab his knee and call for a time-out.

But he felt calmer as he repeated after the preacher.

"Now, here's the really important part," the preacher said, as he provided Noel with the words that pledged his faithfulness to Ryla.

The preacher did not know them personally, so he had no way of knowing that the pledge of faithfulness would be most important to Ryla. As Noel repeated the words, Ryla started to tear up. He wanted to wrap her in his arms and wipe each tear away, but it was time for Ryla to leave him again.

As Noel thought about Ryla running down that aisle away from him and all that could have been between them, he wanted to kick himself for being such an idiot and not figuring out a way to forgive Ryla so the three of them could be a family.

The preacher turned to Ryla and said, "Repeat these words after me."

Noel closed his eyes, not wanting to watch Ryla walk out of his life again.

The preacher said, "I, Ryla Evans, take you, Noel Carter, to be my wedded husband."

Noel not only had his eyes closed, he was holding his breath, waiting for the moment when Ryla would call the wedding off and run out of here.

But instead, he heard, "I, Ryla Evans, take you, Noel Carter, to be my wedded husband."

What was happening? What did he miss? Noel opened his eyes and stared at Ryla as she pledged to stick with him through sickness and in health, "till death do us part." He turned to Ian, who stood as one of his best men along with his brother. But Ian appeared as confused as he.

Noel looked at the preacher as he quoted the "I will be faithful" line. He turned back to Ryla, waiting for her to say something like "Just kidding," and then start running, but instead he saw the tears in her eyes. Her voice broke as she tightened the hold on his hands and repeated the last line.

His eyes were blinking, trying to telegraph a "what are you doing?" message to her, while the tears in her eyes and the look on her face implored for him to understand. He didn't understand this at all.

CHAPTER 18

"You may now kiss your bride."

Ryla saw Noel hesitate and she started chewing her bottom lip. Had she overplayed her hand? What if he rejected her in front of all two hundred of their closest friends and family?

Noel slowly leaned forward and lowered his head until their lips touched. The kiss was soft and sweet, nothing like the hunger Noel normally displayed when he kissed her. When their lips parted, he glared at her for the briefest moment and then came up smiling as if he'd just won a gold medal.

The penetrating glare they'd just shared made her wonder if she'd just won the battle only to lose the war of love. She squeezed his hand, trying to communicate her love for him.

The preacher then told them to turn around and face their guests. Once they had done so, he said, "Ladies and gentlemen, I present to you Mr. and Mrs. Noel Jaylen Carter."

Noel used his free hand to pick up Jaylen and the three of them strolled down the aisle together, as a family. For that brief moment in time, Ryla was truly happy. They stood in the receiving line, shook hands and gave hugs just like any other newly married couple would do. However, Ryla kept her eyes averted from Noel's. She would probably burst out in tears if he glared at her again.

"Ryla you look simply beautiful . . . marvelous."

"And Noel, you are quite handsome."

The guests were showering them with so much love and attention that Ryla began to relax and enjoy the fact that she was now Mrs. Noel Carter — that was, until Danetta approached and said, "You didn't have that talk with Noel, did you?"

"Don't rain on my wedding day, Danetta, not now!"

Danetta grabbed her arm and moved her off to the side. "It's about to storm on your wedding day. Girl, haven't you noticed the looks Noel has been giving you when he thinks no one is looking?"

Ryla waved off the notion of Noel being upset. "He'll be fine once we get through the honeymoon. I have a lot planned for us."

"I just wish you would have thought this through," Danetta said while rubbing her temples, the stress showing on her face.

"Well, no one is as perfect as you, Danetta. But guess what? I still like my life just the way it is. So back off, okay?"

Raising her hands, Danetta said, "Hey, I'm on your side. I just want you to be happy."

Ryla wrapped her arms around her friend and hugged her. As they pulled apart, she kissed Danetta on the cheek. "I know you only have my best interests at heart, but be happy for me. Because I am so happy, okay?"

Danetta nodded.

"Are you and Marshall prepared to babysit Jaylen tomorrow?"

Danetta smiled. "We're actually very excited for the opportunity. I plan to pick Jaylen up from your mom's house early tomorrow morning, and then I'll take her to breakfast and to the mall."

"She'll love it. Thanks." Ryla walked away to join Noel and the rest of their guests in the ballroom. As she headed toward the bridal table, Ryla heard her guests commenting on how lovely the room was. It had been her dream to have her wedding at the Four Seasons, and Noel had made it all possible. She would have to figure out some way to thank him.

Noel was already seated as she approached the table. Dinner was being served. He stood and helped her into her chair, but right away turned back to a conversation he was having with Ian.

Ian was saying, "I'm glad you finally listened to me and left the surprise factor out of the wedding, if you know what I mean."

"Ryla is full of surprises, all right," Noel responded, and then picked up his fork and started shoving food in his mouth.

Jaylen skipped to the table and hugged her mom and dad. "We did it," she said. "We're a real family now."

Noel visibly winced.

Ryla had thought that Noel would come around and see that their marriage was the best thing for both of them. What was she going to do if Noel refused to work with her? "Yes, baby, we're a real family now," Ryla affirmed.

The DJ called out for the first dance of the evening. A dance meant for husband and wife. Ryla glanced over at her husband. He had already stood and extended his hand to her. She sighed in relief as she walked out onto the dance floor with him, while Etta James crooned "At Last." Ryla put her head on Noel's shoulder and swayed with the music. Everything was going to work out — it had to, because her love had finally come back, and he was hers . . . at last.

Noel leaned his head down and whispered to her, "I don't care how beautiful you are. I'll never let you destroy me again."

What was he talking about? She didn't want to destroy him; she wanted to care for him. Didn't he know . . . ? Couldn't he see in her eyes how much she loved him?

"I'm not trying to destroy you, Noel. I only want the best for you and us."

"Then annul this farce of a marriage. I don't care if I lose this election, because soon enough you'll walk out on me. Just do it and get it over with."

But annulling her marriage was the last thing on Ryla's mind. She had plans to show Noel just how good they could be together if he would just give her a chance. She took her head off his shoulder and looked him in the eye. "Can't you see that this way is better for us?"

"Better for us? Or better for you, because once again you are doing exactly what you want, regardless of my wishes."

"We're married, Noel. Don't you remember? This is our dream. Dance with me and let's just enjoy the moment."

The song ended and Noel dropped his arms and walked off the dance floor. Ryla was about to follow him, but then her father tapped her on the shoulder.

"It's my turn," Ryan said with a nervous grin on his face.

"Sure." Ryla reluctantly took her father's hand and allowed him to guide her around the dance floor. It was truly a magical day. Noel would come around — Ryla was sure of it. He was the man of her dreams and she didn't want to imagine a world without him in it. But she did admit to herself that things might be a bit better between them if she had talked to him before the ceremony. So they could have been on the same page concerning the whole "I do" process.

Better for us? How could she possibly think that tricking him into marrying her would be better than being honest and up front? Ryla was always going to be Ryla, and Noel needed a drink.

"You did it." Donald slapped Noel on the back. "My little brother is all grown up now. I guess you won't need me anymore."

His brother somehow always showed up at just the right time. Because if he had been another second later, Noel would have been over at the bar, downing shots as he would ice-cold water on a hot summer day. "Yeah, I guess I did it."

Donald's brow furrowed in confusion. "What's with the frown? You've got a beautiful wife and a wonderful little girl. We should be celebrating rather than looking so sad."

"Thanks, bro, I'll take that into consideration." Noel walked away from his brother only to run into Ian.

"Well, you've got the wife. Now all we have to do is win this election."

Noel had made a point to enjoy his engagement, because he hadn't thought there would be a marriage. Now everyone wanted him to enjoy a marriage that never should have taken place. He raised his hand and halfheartedly said, "Whoo-hoo."

The smile dropped from Ian's face. "It'll get better, man. She's a good woman."

After that Noel was like a robot. He cut the cake, laughed and talked with guests, performed a few line dances and spent the rest of the night dancing with Ryla. He then stood at the door, shaking hands and saying good-night, as guests left the ballroom.

Ryla and Jaylen sauntered over to him. Jaylen laid her head against his leg. "I'm tired, Daddy."

"Of course you're tired — it's past your bedtime."

Ryla put her arm in his. "I'm getting sleepy, too. Do you wanna go up to our suite?"

She had played him like a fiddle the entire time. Noel now felt like a fool for inviting her to come up to his suite once everything with the wedding was over and done. He had been trying to tell her that he wouldn't mind rekindling a little somethin' somethin', while she had known that she didn't need an invitation. As Mrs. Noel Carter, she had access to every room in their suite.

Noel had to hand it to her — the girl had skills. But he could see in her lust-filled eyes what she wanted from him tonight. He had asked her for an annulment, but now Noel knew that Ryla had no intention of following those instructions, either. But he wasn't the one to be tricked. His mother always said, "Fool me once, shame on you. Fool me twice, shame on me." Game on, as far as Noel was concerned. "Yes, Mrs. Carter, I am ready to go to our suite."

"Let me take Jaylen back to my mother and then we can head on up." She lifted an eyebrow, giving him a suggestive look.

Noel grabbed hold of Jaylen and said, "Baby girl, don't you want to see where your mom and dad will be staying for the weekend before you go off with your grandmother?"

"Yes, Daddy. Mommy said you are staying in the president's room."

Ryla laughed. "No, baby, I said that we're staying in the Presidential Suite. The room doesn't belong to the actual president."

"Then why do they call it the Presidential Suite?"

"It's just a way of saying that it's the best room they have. The room is fit for a princess, like you." Noel touched his daughter's nose with his finger. He then grabbed her hand. "Come on, let's go up to the room."

Ryla put her hand on Noel's shoulder. "Baby, I'm sorry but we won't have time to give Jaylen a tour of the room. My mom is ready to go home. And I doubt that she'll want to wait on Jaylen."

"That's fine," Noel said nonchalantly. "Jaylen can spend the night with us. You'd like that, wouldn't you, honey?"

"I'd love it." Jaylen started dancing around the ballroom.

Noel was almost giddy inside as he watched Ryla's face drop. Evidently, she thought he was too dumb to catch on to the little game she was playing. But he was about to show her how champions played the game.

CHAPTER 19

Noel thought he was slick, but Ryla had his number. She wasn't about to let anything else get in between the consummation of their wedding vows. While Noel was giving Jaylen a tour of the suite, Ryla called her mother.

"Hey, sweetie, I'm getting tired. Is Jaylen ready to go?" Juanita asked when she answered the phone.

"I'm getting ready to soak in the tub. Why don't you give Noel five more minutes with Jaylen and then come and get her."

"Will do."

"Thanks, Mom. We appreciate what you're doing for us," Ryla said and then hung up the phone. She hummed as she went into the luxurious bathroom and ran a bubble bath for herself.

Ryla leaned her head back against the base of the tub and allowed the jets to take her away. The day had been full of so many emotions and so much activity that her muscles were tight and truly needed that massage that she and Noel would be getting the next day. Even though the jets were soothing her aching muscles, Ryla only allowed herself about fifteen minutes in the tub. This was, after all, her honeymoon night.

Her bags had been brought to the room earlier in the day, when Noel thought she'd be hiding out here with him, giving him the weekend of a lifetime without the benefit of marriage. She almost giggled as she thought about that day, but it was possible that Noel was waiting for her in the bedroom, so she finished up in the bath and hurried out.

She towel-dried herself and then layered her body with a Christian Dior fragranced body lotion. Ryla then slipped into the silky white number she'd bought to drive Noel out of his mind with desire. She put a silk robe on over her gown. But just before she opened the bathroom door, she changed her mind, took the robe off and left it in the bathroom.

Strutting into the bedroom, Ryla struck a pose in front of the bed. It was at that moment she noticed that the bed was empty. "Where is he?" she mused as she began to search over the thousand-square-foot suite.

She soon found Noel and Jaylen sleeping on the sofa in front of the television. Noel was stretched out on the couch, while Jaylen lay on his chest. They were sleeping so soundly that Ryla almost hated the thought of waking them, but this was her honeymoon night.

Standing next to the headrest, she nudged Noel and then whispered in his ear.

Noel jumped, almost tossing Jaylen onto the floor. He grabbed her and held on as he focused his eyes on Ryla. "What time is it?"

"It's midnight." Ryla pointed at Jaylen and whispered, "My mom was supposed to get her. Let me go call her."

"Don't worry about it." Noel sat up. "Your mom came to pick her up, but Jaylen wanted to spend the night with us, so I told her to go on home."

So that's how it's going to be, huh? She stood in front of him so he could get a full view of the way her beautiful silky gown clung to her body. She watched his eyes travel the distance. Ryla smiled, because it was obvious that he liked everything his eyes beheld.

"You ready for bed?" he asked.

Ryla put her hands to her neck and rolled it around as if she was massaging it. But what she was really doing was trying to give

Noel another free look at her form. When she turned back to him, she said, "I've been ready for bed for hours."

"Is that right?"

"Mmmph." She was looking him in the eye, trying to transmit some I-really-want-to-be-with-you signals.

Noel stood, picked Jaylen up and slung her over his shoulder. "Well, let's all go to bed then."

"What?" Ryla grabbed Noel's arm. "You are not really considering taking Jaylen to our bed tonight?"

He turned to her with a clueless expression on his face. "Oh, do you not want me to put her in bed with us?"

"It's our honeymoon. Are you crazy?" She put her hands on her hips and declared, "No, I certainly don't want Jaylen to sleep with us tonight."

"Good. I'm glad you got that off your chest." He then walked past her, went into their bedroom and laid Jaylen in the middle of the bed. Noel then grabbed his pajamas out of the dresser drawer and walked off toward the bathroom.

"Why are you doing this, Noel? This is our wedding night."

His hand was on the doorknob as he flung back, "In this family we do exactly what we want, and nothing that anyone else wants, remember?"

Noel didn't sleep well. Jaylen kept jabbing him in the gut and Ryla's perfume was doing a number on him, causing him to think of things a husband wanted to do with his wife. But he reminded himself who he was, and that he had conquered bigger problems than this in his thirty-two years on earth. Ryla wouldn't win this fight.

He punched his pillow, flopped around on the bed and then willed himself to sleep. When this weekend was over, Ryla would be filing for an annulment, and that would be that.

By morning, Noel had a crook in his neck and was so tired from being jabbed and pushed that he wanted to keep his eyes closed for another hour. But sunlight was beaming through the room. And Noel noticed something else. Jaylen wasn't asleep beside him any longer.

He opened his eyes and sat up in bed. The blinds were open and no one was in bed with him. Noel threw the covers off and went in search of his little girl.

Ryla was humming as she strutted around, watering the flowers that were set on tables around the suite. She had taken off the silky white nightgown that had clung to her like a second skin. Now she was in stilettos and a hunter-green gown that ended just above her knee. It wasn't as sexy as the gown she had worn last night, but Noel had to admit, those stilettos set it off. "Where's Jaylen?" he asked, hoping that his little girl would come to her daddy's rescue.

"Danetta picked her up already." She put the water pitcher down and said, "Breakfast is on the terrace. What would you like to drink this morning? I ordered orange juice and apple juice. But if you'd like something else, I can have it brought up."

She was playing her lady-of-the-manor role to the hilt, but Noel wasn't interested. "Why did you allow your friend to take my daughter without consulting me?"

"Why did you bring *our* daughter to the room last night without consulting me?" she threw back at him.

Noel rolled his eyes upward. "I'm done with this conversation. I'm going to eat my breakfast and then pack my bags."

She followed him out to the terrace and sat down across from him. As he piled ham, bacon, eggs and breakfast potatoes onto his plate, Ryla said, "We need to talk about what's going on between us."

Noel began wolfing the food down like a

hungry refugee. "Nothing's between us but Jaylen. So, unless she is what you want to talk about, I'm not interested."

Ryla held up her left hand. "I am your wife, you know."

"Not my fault," he said as he kept eating.

"What's wrong with you? Why are you acting this way?" Her voice took on a pleading note.

Noel finished his food, wiped his mouth and then asked, "What day would you like to meet to file for the annulment?"

"Why are you being so unreasonable?"

"Why didn't you follow the plan?"

Shaking her head and blowing out hot air, she stood. "This isn't getting us anywhere." She left the terrace.

Noel got up and followed her back into the suite. "Don't walk away from me, dear wife. I thought you wanted to talk. So let's have it." He grabbed her arm and turned her around to face him. "You were supposed to call this wedding off yesterday, so why didn't you? How could you even stand there and repeat those vows to me?"

"You know why I did it."

"No, I don't." He pointed a finger at himself and started jabbing himself in the chest with every word. "Yesterday was one of the hardest days of my life. Because I knew I was going to be reciting vows that I meant." He turned his pointer finger on her. "But you stood there repeating those sacred words even though you didn't mean any of them."

"I meant every word of my vows to you," she shot back.

"That's a bold-faced lie, and you know it."

"Why would I continue on with the ceremony if I didn't mean those words . . . if I didn't want to be married to you?"

"I have no idea why you do the things you do, but I do know that you didn't mean those words. Or you never would have run off eight years ago." He ran his hand over his hair, sighed and continued. "You would have told me about my baby and we would have gotten married a long time ago."

"I thought you were cheating on me. I could never have married a cheater and I certainly didn't want my child fathered by one."

He was angry now. In two long strides he closed the distance between them. "You should have asked me about it. You don't just run off with a man's child and never say a word to him about it. What kind of person are you?"

He could tell that she was itching to

scratch his eyes out. But instead, she took a deep breath and said, "I'm the mother of your child and I am the woman you married."

"You're the woman I was tricked into marrying," Noel threw back, as he headed for the bedroom.

"Where are you going?"

"To pack," he flung over his shoulder.

Ryla marched into their bedroom. "You are not going to leave me during our honeymoon."

He opened his mouth to say something, but she cut him off. "You told me to enjoy the journey during our engagement. I have done everything you asked, from uprooting Jaylen and myself from our life in Houston, to planning a pretend wedding with you. So now all I'm asking is that you let me have my honeymoon."

He wanted to reject her flat out. But as he considered what she said, he had to admit that Ryla had a small point. She hadn't given him much of a fuss with anything he'd asked her to do. He put his clothes back in the drawer and decided to hear her out. "What's on the agenda for the day?" Noel said, still slightly irritated.

Ryla jovially clapped her hands. "Well, breakfast was first on the agenda." She

218

pointed toward the terrace. "You've already finished off yours. The next thing . . ."

The doorbell rang. Ryla smiled. "I'll be right back."

Noel flopped down on the bed as he tried to figure a way out of the trap that Ryla was surely setting for him. If things had turned out differently for them, Noel would be floating around the hotel room, thrilled that he was finally married to the woman of his dreams.

But Ryla had deceived him. She had hurt him in a way that he couldn't conceive of getting over anytime soon, no matter how hard he tried.

Ryla popped her head into the bedroom. "The second thing on our agenda is here, so come on into the living room."

Reluctantly, Noel followed Ryla. When he entered the living room, he noticed that the furniture had been pushed back and two massage tables had been placed in the empty space. He turned to Ryla and said, "I don't think couple's massages are such a good thing this weekend."

"Come on, baby, you need this." Ryla grabbed his arm and moved him over to one of the massage tables. "You've been working hard on the campaign and on the planning of the wedding with me. We need to loosen those muscles so you can relax."

Maybe Ryla was right. The stress of the campaign had been wearing on him. "Okay, let's do it," Noel said as he leaned against the table.

The masseuses gathered their materials and then instructed Noel and Ryla to take off their clothes and lie down under the covers.

Ryla stood and began undressing in front of him as if she'd spent a lifetime doing it. Noel wanted to change his mind. A massage *was* a bad idea . . . a really bad idea.

CHAPTER 20

Ryla had a whole day of events planned for them. After the massage, they went to the pool for a swim. Lunch was served to them poolside. And she enjoyed every minute of it, because Noel was once again on his best behavior.

"So, what's on the agenda after this?"

"We have a few hours of free time, so we can read a book, or we can go to our room and take a nap together. What do you think?" As she said the words, she was leaning toward him, giving him ample view of everything her two-piece swimsuit didn't cover.

"Free time sounds good." Noel took a sip of his iced tea. "You go ahead and take that nap — I'm going to the business center to check my emails."

"Noel, you're on your honeymoon. Why on earth would you waste time checking emails?"

He put his drink down and with a stone face told her, "This is *your* honeymoon, Ryla. You made all of these plans, so I hope you enjoy them." He stood. "I'm going to get a little work done."

"Okay, but don't be too long. We have an event-filled evening," she called after him, trying to keep her enthusiasm up as he exited the pool area.

He waved his acknowledgment of her words, but kept walking.

Ryla slumped back into her lounge chair. She only had this night left to convince Noel that they should stay married. But he was not helping at all. Maybe she'd been wrong for assuming that Noel still loved and cared for her. Maybe she should give up before she made an even bigger fool of herself.

Ryla went back to her big lonely suite, took her e-reader out of her purse and began reading a romance novel until she drifted off to sleep. In her dreamland, she and Noel were walking on the beach, hand in hand. They came to the spot where they had left their blanket and Noel sat down and pulled Ryla into his loving arms.

He hungrily kissed her and Ryla kissed him right back, not caring who saw them on the beach. They were in love and they needed each other.

"Wake up, Ryla." Noel nudged her.

Ryla shot up as if an alarm had gone off.

"You were moaning. You must have been dreaming something hot and heavy," Noel said with devilment in his eyes.

"That's for me to know and for you to want to find out," she said as she scooted off the bed. "What time is it?"

"A little after five."

Ryla became frantic. "I slept that long! Oh, my goodness. I need to shower."

"What's going on?" Noel asked.

"We have dinner plans. I need to get dressed." She ran into the bathroom and jumped in the shower. *Don't mess this up — this is your last chance with Noel.* She planned to walk out of this hotel, hand in hand with her husband tomorrow morning. So she needed to work it tonight.

When she got out of the shower, she put lotion over her body and then threw on a strapless lavender-and-black evening gown that accentuated her curves and complemented her honey-toned complexion. She just hoped she would be able to get Noel to take notice of her, since nothing else she'd worn this weekend seemed to do anything for him.

She entered the living room just as the doorbell rang. Noel was seated on the sofa, watching television. "I'll get it," he said.

"No, no. You just go and get ready. I'll take care of everything out here."

When he turned toward her, she noticed the appreciation in his eyes for what she was wearing. There was hope.

"So, I need to put on something dressy for tonight, huh?"

"Please, if you don't mind."

"Okay, I'll be out in twenty," he said casually.

"Make it thirty," she said as she opened the door. Two waiters stood behind the door; one was pushing a cartload of food, and the other carried linens for the table. Ryla directed them to the dining room table, as if they hadn't been there and done this a hundred times or more for other guests.

Three musicians stood directly behind the waiters. One carried a flute, one, a violin and the other, a cello. "Come in, gentlemen. And thank you for being timely."

"It's your honeymoon," one of them said. "We would never make a bride wait."

She wished Noel felt the same way. "Thank you for being so kind to us."

She went back to the bedroom to give everyone time to set up. Noel was still in the shower. She noted the black suit and lavender shirt that he'd laid out on the bed. She smiled at his effort.

She wrote a note, asking him to meet her in the dining room, then left the note on top of his shirt. Ryla went back out to make sure the setup was moving along. She had ordered lobster, garlic potatoes and asparagus. The linen had been put on the table with a fresh bouquet of roses. As she leaned over and smelled them, she remembered how Noel had filled her aunt's porch with rose petals the night he proposed to her.

She took the roses out of the vase and began sprinkling the rose petals in front of their bedroom door so that Noel would be walking on the petals as he entered the room. She continued sprinkling her trail of rose petals from the bedroom door all the way to the dining room table.

"Ah, madam, you are a true romantic," one of the musicians said.

"Thank you," she said, as the waiter handed her the vanilla-scented candles she had asked them to bring. Ryla set the candles in candleholders that she'd placed around the room earlier that day. As the waiter lit the candles, she dimmed the lights.

By the time she finished setting the mood in the room, the waiters were putting dinner on the table, and the musicians began to softly serenade her. The bedroom door opened, and Ryla turned and watched as her man sauntered over to the table and stood in front of her.

His eyes danced over the room. He swayed a bit to the music. "When did you plan all of this?"

"Right after you invited me to spend the weekend here with you."

He stepped back, looked at everything again and then gave her another once-over. "You've done well."

"I'm glad you like." She grabbed her chair, getting ready to pull it out.

Noel removed her hand from the chair. "Excuse me," he told her as he pulled the chair out, allowed her to sit in it and then pushed it up to the table. "I think this is my job."

"What's got you being such a gentleman?"

Noel sat, and the waiter put napkins in his and Ryla's laps. "If you can go through all this trouble, the least I can do is be civil."

No, the least you could do is love me like you once did. She nodded and then asked, "Would you like to say grace?"

"Certainly," he said as he grabbed hold of her hands and prayed.

They then ate their meal and enjoyed pleasant conversation, while the music serenaded them. Ryla was having such a good time with Noel that she forgot that she needed to try to win him over with this meal — rather, she found comfort in being herself. This was Noel, after all, and if anyone knew her, he did.

She had hoped that he would ask her to dance when they finished eating. But as they continued to sit and talk while the music played, Ryla thought she'd have to take matters into her own hands. "Would you like to dance?"

Noel peered over at the musicians and then turned back to Ryla. "I guess we should. I mean, we don't want them to think we didn't enjoy the music." Noel stood and held out his hand for Ryla.

"Thank you, sir." She took his hand and waltzed onto the makeshift dance floor with him.

As he put his arm around her and began to sway to the music, the song changed and suddenly they were dancing to the instrumental version of "At Last." Noel leaned back and looked at Ryla. "Did you tell them to do that?"

"It is our song, baby." Her hands were caressing his back as they continued to sway to the music. "We danced to this song last night in front of a roomful of people. But I want you to know, in the privacy of our room, that I'm glad that you are finally mine . . . *at last.*" She sang those last two words into his ear and felt him melt a little in her arms.

When that song finished, Noel held on to her as the music switched to the instrumental version of another love song. "This is nice. I wish I had thought of it."

"You came up with some good dates, so I wanted to take care of the honeymoon." Leaning her head against his chest, she felt his heart beat faster, and she knew that she was getting to him. He was beginning to see her as the woman he not only had married, but desired.

She lifted her head and asked, "Do you want me to send everyone away?" *Please say yes . . . please say yes,* she silently chanted.

He released her so quickly she had to grab onto the table or risk falling on her backside.

"L-let me get my wallet so I can give them a tip," Noel stammered as he rushed to their bedroom. He came back out carrying several bills. He handed them off to the musicians and the waiters.

One of the waiters said, "We'll clean this up before we go."

"Oh, no," Noel said, "just leave it. And

someone can get it tomorrow." He walked them to the door and quickly closed it behind them.

"Noel, don't push the people out like that," Ryla said while laughing at him.

As Noel turned back around and looked at Ryla, he knew he was a goner, but at that moment he just didn't care anymore. He would wave the white flag, throw in the towel — whatever he had to do to be with Ryla tonight. His long legs carried him back to the middle of the room where she stood and he said, "I promised myself that I would never make love to you again. Loving you has taken too much from me."

She reached up and gently stroked his face. "Noel, please believe me when I say that you don't have to fear loving me. I won't ever hurt you again. I promise."

His head lowered and, before either of them knew it was happening, their lips met and, without any music, they slowly began the seductive dance of love. Growling his impatience, Noel swept her in his arms. With the precision of a soldier under military orders, he marched into their bedroom, where his strong arms released her onto the bed as if she were a precious stone. Then he seemed to release the male hunger within him as he tugged off his jacket and flung it to the floor. "God help me, Ryla, I tried to stay away from you, but I can't. I just can't."

His voice sounded so tortured. Ryla lifted from the bed and pulled him down with her, wanting to love the pain away. "And I can't forgive myself for destroying our love unless you forgive me. I need you to forget all the bad memories of the past, Noel. Let this night be about consummating our new love."

Noel didn't answer as he began to love Ryla as if it was the very first time for both of them. His caresses were tender and his kisses soft and unrushed. Then they experienced a night like no other, as husband and wife.

CHAPTER 21

Stretching and yawning, Ryla woke to a new day. She and Noel had shared a wonderful night of lovemaking and she wanted to spend the morning doing the same. Even though she was waking up, she was still too tired to open her eyes. Reaching over to wake Noel, Ryla's hand went farther and farther to the other side of the bed until she opened her eyes and saw for herself that the bed was empty.

She sat up, pulling the sheet with her. Noel was gone, but there was an envelope with her name on it on his pillow. Ryla was afraid to pick the envelope up. Why wasn't Noel in bed with her? She hoped and prayed she wasn't about to open that envelope and find cash and a thank-you note for a good time.

Against her better judgment, she picked up the envelope and pulled the notecard out of it. Noel's handwriting was recognizable to her immediately.

Ryla, I need to get some things done
back in Dallas. Please go to your house
in Houston and I will contact you when
the campaign is over so I can set up
visitation with Jaylen.

Did Noel just break up with her? Did he
really leave her a Dear Ryla card? She
jumped out of bed and walked every inch
of the suite in hope that Noel was still there.
But the suite was empty.

"How could he do this?" she wondered
out loud. "How could he just leave me like
last night meant nothing?"

He'd told her that he didn't want to marry
her, but she'd gone through with her crazy
scheme to win him back anyway. And what
did it get her? A husband who didn't even
want her in the same city with him. She col-
lapsed down on the bed and let the river of
tears flow.

Was this how it felt for Noel when she left
him? Yes, Ryla knew that she had wronged
him by walking away as she had, but she
had been a high-strung teenager, with issues. If she hadn't been so young and naive,
Ryla was quite sure that she would have
seen that Noel was nothing like her cheat-

ing father.

After emptying a box of tissues, Ryla grabbed the toilet paper from the bathroom and blew her nose. She then lay back down and cried until she realized it was noon and she was supposed to check out an hour ago. She pulled herself out of bed, walked around the room, picking up clothes that had been discarded last night. She threw her suitcase on the bed and filled it with her things.

After zipping her suitcase, she checked the dresser to make sure that Noel hadn't left any of his clothes behind. When she saw that the drawers were empty, Ryla's eyes began to tear up again.

Her eyes were red and swollen, so she took her sunglasses out of her purse and put them on. She looked around the room one last time to make sure she wasn't leaving anything, grabbed her suitcase and then left the beautiful suite, alone. Ryla tried her best not to cry as she exited the Four Seasons, but the tears came anyway.

She wanted to just go home and get in her fetal position in her bed and stay that way until her life made sense again. But she had to pick up Jaylen. So she drove to Danetta's house to get her little girl. She wished she could just honk the horn and that Jaylen would come running out, but she knew Danetta wouldn't go for any foolishness like that. So Ryla got out of the car and rang her friend's doorbell.

Danetta answered the door, saying, "I see you and Noel took your sweet time leaving the hotel."

Ryla stepped in and drily said, "I didn't feel like leaving earlier. I hope I didn't mess up any plans that you had."

"Of course not, girl, I was just messing with you. Marshall went to work already. Jaylen and I were just hanging around the house."

"Can you get her so I can get going, please?"

Danetta started to walk away, but then turned back to her friend. "Are you okay?"

Nodding, Ryla said, "Yeah, I'm fine. I'm just ready to go home."

Danetta hollered for Jaylen. "Your mom is here, so hurry up." She then looked back at Ryla. "Are you sure you don't want to sit down?"

Waving away the gesture, Ryla said, "No, I'm just ready to go home. I have a splitting headache."

Jaylen came running into the foyer. She screamed, "Mommy!" but then stopped and began looking around. She turned back to her mother and said, "Where is Daddy? I thought we were going back to Dallas with him."

"Not right now, honey. Daddy has some very important business to take care of." She tried to sound like the normal, happy, chipper event planner that she was as she added, "He can't very well entertain us while he's trying to win an election, now, can he?"

With a dejected look on her face, Jaylen reminded her mother, "Daddy wants me with him. He said that the campaign wasn't any fun until I arrived. I need to get to Dallas, Mommy, because my daddy is going to miss me."

Chewing her bottom lip and rubbing her temple to relieve some of the stress and strain she was feeling, Ryla tried to think of an answer for her daughter. Maybe she and Jaylen should just go on back to Dallas. Who did Noel think he was, relegating her to one side of Texas while he took the other side?

Danetta put her hand on Jaylen's shoulder and said, "Baby, go get all of your stuff. Auntie Danetta needs to speak with your mommy for a moment."

Jaylen skipped her way to the stairs. As she climbed them, Ryla held up a hand of defense. "I can't go through this right now."

"Stop hiding behind those sunglasses." Danetta reached up and pulled the glasses from her friend's face. Danetta gasped. "What's wrong, Ryla? Why have you been crying like this?"

Ryla pulled her glasses out of Danetta's hand and put them back on. "Let's just say you were right and I was way off base. Are you happy now?"

"You know I'm not." Danetta continued to look her friend over and then asked, "Did you and Noel have a big fight or something?"

"No, Noel doesn't fight with people who don't matter to him."

"What happened, Ryla? Talk to me."

"I can't do this." Ryla rushed over to the door and grabbed hold of the doorknob. "Tell Jaylen to meet me in the car. I'll talk to you later, okay?"

Danetta nodded and then patted her friend on the back as she exited.

Like a firestorm, Noel blazed into his campaign headquarters ready to get down to business and put this election behind him. "Good morning." He waved at his staff as he passed them on his way to his office. Before Noel could close his door, Ian had come into his office and closed the door for him.

"What are you doing here so early?"

Noel glanced at his watch. "I don't know how getting here at ten in the morning is considered early."

"You know what I mean. I wouldn't have expected you to be out of bed so soon." Grinning as if he had knowledge of a well-kept secret, he added, "I mean, you are a honeymooner."

Noel sat behind his desk. "I'm a honeymooner with an election to win. So, if you don't mind, I would appreciate it if we could get off my personal life and get back our focus on winning this election."

Ian shrugged. "I'm fine with getting out of your personal business. But I have a little personal business of my own that I need your help with."

Happy to talk about anything but the wedding, Noel perked up and said, "What can I help you with?"

"I need a phone number for one of Ryla's bridesmaids."

The wedding again. "I was only introduced to Ryla's friends a few times. But I do know that one is married."

"I'm talking about Surry. I tried to talk to her at the wedding, but she sort of blew me

237

off. But I figured I would give her a call and see where I stand."

Noel wanted to tell his friend to run — don't get involved with anyone associated with Ryla. But he wouldn't let his own bitterness spoil it for Ian. "I'll see what I can do. Now, can you tell me where we stand in the polls?"

"I had Cathy gathering that information. But since I didn't think you'd actually show up today, I told her not to rush it." Ian headed for the door. "Let me check on those figures."

"And can you see if anybody has some Tylenol or something?" He put his hands to his head and rubbed his temples. "My head is killing me."

Ian left the office and Noel was left with his thoughts of last night with Ryla. It had been a beautiful experience to be with her again. Ryla had been loving and giving, but as he woke early this morning and looked down at his sleeping beauty, his heart raced, his pulse quickened as sweat began to drip from his forehead.

He was having a panic attack. His only thought was to get out of that bed and as far away from Ryla as possible. They had too many issues to ever be able to make a marriage work. He threw his clothes into his suitcase and then wrote her a note. But as he was heading out the door of their suite, he suddenly felt like the runner he'd accused her of being.

As he stood by the door, thinking about going back to his wife, a vision of her one day walking out the door and leaving him tore at his will. Why was he in love with a woman who could so easily discard him? Noel had no answers for his weakness, but he didn't have to succumb to it. He opened the door and left the suite. Noel wished he could say that he didn't look back. But that wasn't the truth. The entire way to his car, Noel kept looking back, wondering if Ryla would realize he was gone and try to stop him.

A knock on his door brought Noel's attention back to the events of the day. "Come in."

Cathy walked through the door carrying a folder in one hand and a bottle of Tylenol in the other. She set the folder on his desk. "Good morning."

"Good morning, yourself," he said, reaching for the pain pills.

She grabbed him a bottle of water from the top of his file cabinet, opened it and handed it to him. "You look stressed," she said, as Noel plopped three pills in his mouth.

"You don't know the half of it," he said, and then pointed at the folder. "Is this the polling information from this weekend?"

"Sure is, buddy, and your numbers are up." Cathy clapped and then added in a gleeful tone, "So I guess that whole marry-your-baby's-mama stunt worked out for you, huh?"

Noel looked up from the poll numbers he'd been studying. "What?"

She winked at him. "You don't have to pretend with me. I saw how you treated Ryla when she and Jaylen first arrived. So I knew that you didn't want anything to do with her. And the fact that you're back in the office so soon after your wedding speaks for itself, don't you think?"

Ryla had been right about Cathy all along. She was one of those women who would stop at nothing to break up a family. He stood and addressed the issue. "I'm married, Cathy, and I love my wife. End of story."

She stammered. "W-well, I — I just thought . . ."

"You thought wrong. And I think it's time for you to go. I appreciate all the work you've done for this campaign, but Ryla feels uncomfortable with you being here. And I have to agree with her."

With a look of astonishment on her face, she asked, "You're firing me?"

Noel sat back down. "You can give your letter of resignation to Ian and then pack your things. You shouldn't have any trouble finding another campaign to work for, because you were an excellent *employee.*" He stressed the word.

"Don't worry, Noel. I won't say anything to the media about how you planned your marriage to get your poll numbers to rise." She sneered and then added, "And how pathetic Ryla is for going along with your scheme. You two deserve each other." Cathy turned and huffed out of his office.

Noel didn't know if Cathy's statement about him and Ryla deserving each other was true, but he did know one thing. He needed a drink.

CHAPTER 22

Ryla had been in bed all week, refusing to shower or even change her clothes. Her mother had come by a couple of times a day to make either soup or sandwiches for Jaylen. After the third day, however, Juanita entered her bedroom, closed the door and then sat down on the edge of her bed.

Ryla put the cover over her head, because she didn't have the energy to deal with her mother right now.

Juanita pulled the cover away from Ryla and said, "I'm not even going to pretend to understand why you would marry that man and then leave him in two days, but —"

Her mother's words snapped her back to life. She interrupted her mother as she jumped up and blurted, "You think I left him? Ha! I wish I had left him. But this time Noel left me with nothing but a note to figure that he wasn't coming back."

A look of confusion crossed Juanita's face.

"But why would he do that to you, honey? He seemed so in love."

Ryla grabbed a pillow and held on to it as she fessed up. "Noel is still holding a grudge against me, Mom. He can't love me, because he's still so angry with me about keeping Jaylen from him."

"But he asked you to marry him."

Ryla hated having to tell her mother what a fool she had been for love. But since she had willingly taken part in the farce, it was time to let her mother in on everything. Tears glistened her eyes as she confessed, "He asked me to pretend to marry him. I'm the one who went all the way with it."

"Oh, Ryla."

Ryla held up a hand, not wanting to deal with the pity she heard in her mother's voice. "I know, Mom. I was a fool to think I could get Noel to love me again."

"No, baby." Juanita shook her head. "Noel's the fool if he could ever stop loving you in the first place."

Touched by her mother's words, Ryla reached out for her mother. The two women hugged.

When Juanita stood back up, she said, "I'm going to take Jaylen home with me for a few days to give you time to cry your eyes out and then pull yourself back together. Okay?"

Ryla nodded. She then watched her mother walk out of her bedroom and listened as she gathered Jaylen's things and left the house. Her little girl hadn't even come into the room to say goodbye, but Ryla didn't blame her. She was a mess, and Jaylen was probably terrified by the sight of her mother.

For the next few days, she tried to follow her mother's advice. But the sad truth was that Ryla didn't know how to pull anything together anymore. Knowledge of that brought laughter to her lips for the first time that week. She was the party planner extraordinaire, known for throwing together fabulous events on short notice. Heck, she'd even put the *fabulous* stamp on her own wedding, with only six weeks to plan. But none of her planning skills would get her out of this deep depression she had fallen into.

Sleep became her friend. No one mocked or judged her while she slept, so Ryla spent her days ignoring the ringing of her telephone as she lay in a comalike state.

Suddenly, her blinds were flung open and Ryla had to pull the covers over her head to keep from being blinded.

"Get up."

Ryla lowered the cover and sent a piercing glare in Danetta's direction. "How did you get in here?"

Danetta held up the key. "I told your mother that I was going to take you to church this morning, and she handed me her spare key. Of course, neither of us believed that you would get out of bed to open the door for me."

"You don't have to sound so rude. I'm going through a traumatic time in my life. Shouldn't I be allowed to wallow around for a few days?"

"A few days, yes. But you haven't gone out of this house since you entered it on Monday. You won't answer the phone and your mother tells me that you haven't combed your hair or changed your clothes in days. And that's not you."

Tears formed in Ryla's eyes. "I really loved him, Danetta. But he doesn't love me anymore." She hit the blanket with her fist. "Maybe I'm not worthy of love after what I did to him."

Danetta searched the room until she found a hand mirror on Ryla's vanity. She sat down on the bed next to Ryla and said, "Look."

Ryla started screaming, "Get that mirror

away from me."

"The mirror isn't going to set you on fire, Ryla. What's wrong with you?" Danetta asked with an arched eyebrow.

"I can't stand to look in these mirrors."

"Since when?" Danetta demanded to know.

Ryla slumped back in her bed and sighed. She had meant to ask Danetta about the man she'd run into at the mall a few months ago, but so much had been going on that she'd never had a chance. But now that her mirror was tormenting her, she needed answers. "I ran into this man at the mall a few months ago. He showed me this little black book that read something like, 'Why did Jesus die?' on the cover. When he opened the book, there was no answer to the question, but a mirror that showed my reflection. It has bothered me ever since, because I don't know what he was trying to say."

"Wow. You've never mentioned this to me," Danetta said.

"I meant to, but life became so busy that I forgot about it, and now I can't get it out of my mind." She looked Danetta in the eye. "Was that man blaming me for demise in general?" Noel blamed her for so much. Maybe others saw the Guilty stamp on her forehead also.

"No, hon, not at all." Danetta smiled. "I wish you had told me about this earlier. Then maybe you wouldn't be such a basket case."

Ryla sniffed. She then grabbed the toilet paper she had been using, since she had run out of tissues, and blew her nose. "I'll probably still be a basket case, but at least I'll feel better about not being blamed for one more thing."

Danetta rushed on with her explanation. "The reason that man showed you a picture of yourself was because he wanted you to know that, if you were the only person on this earth, Jesus still would have bled and died for little ol' you."

"Why?" Ryla asked, as if to say she wasn't worth the effort.

"Because the Lord loves you so much that He even wants to help you get through this terrible time in your life."

"But why? I don't get it."

Ryla had closed herself off from people who hurt or dismissed her, refusing to give them her love to throw around. So the idea of God loving her despite the fact that she hardly went to church or worshipped Him in any meaningful fashion was hard to comprehend.

Danetta held out a hand to her friend. "Come to church with me. Come find out about the God who loves you so dearly."

Ryla had tried to fix things herself and had done a poor job of it for so long that the idea of someone else helping her get where she needed to be intrigued her. She threw the covers back and said, "Why not?"

Ian shook his head as he watched Noel try to right himself on the sofa. He finally gave up and fell face forward into the cushions. Ian opened his cell phone and called Donald. "I hate making this call," Ian said the moment Donald came on the line, "but I picked Noel up at a local bar a little while ago, and he just passed out."

"I'm on my way" was all Donald said, and then he hung up.

Ian walked over to his friend and shoved him. "Did you hear that? I called your brother and he is on the way over here to figure out why you would sabotage your future like this."

Noel lifted his head for a brief moment. "Tell him to bring me a beer." He then fell back into the cushiony softness of his sofa.

The service was wonderful and Ryla was so glad that she'd gotten out of bed to attend church with Danetta and Marshall today. Praise and worship proved to be a magical time for her. Ryla raised her hands, and for the first time in a very long while, she wasn't thinking about what she would get out of praising the Lord. She simply wanted to praise God for the great being that He was.

After the sermon, the pastor asked if anyone wanted to give their life to God. The concept intrigued her. Ryla had never given anything to anyone who hadn't given her something in return. But today would be the day to try something new. She stepped into the aisle and began walking down to the altar. With each step she took, the heaviness of her trials and tribulations seemed to fall off.

As she prayed the sinner's prayer with an altar worker, Ryla felt the weight of unforgiveness fall away. No longer would she hold her father's failings against him. With this newfound ability to forgive, Ryla found that she no longer needed to judge every man by her father's standards. And in finally seeing what she had done to Noel, she realized that she owed him a true apology.

Donald was sitting on the floor with Ian and Noel, force-feeding his brother black coffee and trying to talk some sense into him.

"I love her, man. I really love her," Noel confessed.

"Then why'd you leave her, dummy?" Ian asked, anger flashing in his eyes.

Taking another sip of his coffee, Noel said, "Because I'm exactly what you said — a dummy. And because Ryla has so many issues that she will eventually leave me again. Honestly . . . I just don't know if I can handle her leaving me again."

"You do know that fear doesn't come from God, don't you, bro?" Donald asked.

"Yeah, I know, but this fear has gripped me to the point where I would walk away from the woman I love. Forget the fact that she tricked me into marrying her. I was crazy to be mad about that, because I'd gladly marry Ryla. My problem is that I'd be forever concerned that I might do something to cause her to leave me. I don't want to live like that."

"Do you want to live like this?" Ian pointed at him.

Noel knew that Ian was referring to the fact that he had gotten drunk after being sober for years. "No, I don't want to live like this, either."

Donald got on his knees. "Then pray with me. Let's take your fears to God and then you can go get your woman back."

Donald's idea sounded better than the one Noel had come up with — drinking himself into a coma so he'd stop thinking about Ryla. So he got on his knees and said, "Let's do this."

CHAPTER 23

After the service, Danetta invited Ryla to brunch, but Ryla had other plans. "Thanks, girl, but I'm going to pick Jaylen up from my mom's and then drive to Dallas. I need to talk to Noel."

Danetta smiled. "I'm proud of you, girl. Handle your business."

Ryla hugged Danetta. "Thanks for being my friend. I should have taken your advice in the first place. But I'm learning that God gives us second chances, and I'm hoping that Noel will also."

"He will — just keep the faith."

Oh, she had the faith, all right, and Ryla never wanted to let it go. She picked up Jaylen and put a smile on her child's face when she explained that they were driving to Dallas to see Noel.

She stopped off and purchased some burgers in case Noel was hungry. Every time she had dropped Jaylen off at Noel's house during the summer, it never seemed as if Noel had much food in the cabinets. He was strictly a dining-out kind of man. Noel lived in the high-priced Southlake suburbs of Dallas, where food and amenities were plentiful, so it didn't matter that he didn't cook much.

When they arrived, Ian and Donald were on their way out the door. "You don't have to leave because of us," Ryla told them.

"We don't mind leaving. We've been with your knucklehead husband all morning, and trust me — we need a break."

Ryla laughed. "He's not that bad."

"Yeah, you heard her. I'm not that bad." Noel picked Jaylen up and hugged her. "Hey, little one. I really missed you."

"I told Mommy that you'd be missing me if we didn't come back to Dallas, but she didn't believe me."

"You were right. So don't ever stay away from me this long again."

"I won't," Jaylen assured him, and then wrapped her arms around him again.

Ryla sat quietly as Noel and Jaylen watched cartoons and played silly games. She joined in a few times. But when Jaylen finally fell off to sleep, Ryla turned to Noel and said, "I came here to tell you that I will give you the divorce you want. I never should have tricked you into marrying me. And I don't want you to feel trapped into staying with me."

Dumbfounded, Noel asked, "What happened to change your mind? I mean, when I originally asked for the annulment, you plotted to seduce me instead."

"I attended church today. The message delivered and a little talk I had with Danetta helped me to see that I had been so unfair to you." Tears streamed down her face as she continued to pour out her heart to him. "I lost faith in men after my father left my mother for another woman, and that caused me to spend the last eight years making you pay for what another man did."

"And so, what are you saying — going to church helped you to have faith in me?" Noel asked.

"It wasn't just going to church that did it. It was the message from the pastor on trusting God. It helped me realize that if I put my faith and trust in God, then I don't have to worry about what you may or may not do sometime down the line. I can just trust you, and freely offer you my love. . . . But I also know that this marriage didn't start off right. So, even though I desperately want to be with you, I will let you go. Because I want to do whatever will make you happy."

Noel grabbed hold of her and kissed her with the hunger of a man who had fasted for a month. When he finally released her, he said, "You were right the first time, baby. Being married is definitely better for us."

"Oh, Noel, do you mean it?" Ryla asked with hope springing in her heart.

He kissed her again, trying to show her all the love that was growing in his heart. As they pulled apart, he confessed, "I've been a fool, Ryla. I've never stopped loving you and I would be so very miserable if you left me again."

"Do you think you will ever be able to forgive me for keeping Jaylen from you?"

Nodding as he lightly sprinkled kisses from her forehead to her chin, Noel said, "I don't want to hold any more grudges against you, baby. All I want to do is love you from this day forward. Can you handle that? Do you want to be married to me for real, Ryla Carter?"

She looked at him, and with mischief in her eyes, she said, "I do."

Noel grinned, and as his heart filled with love, he told her, "I do, too, baby. Now and forever."

ABOUT THE AUTHOR

Vanessa Miller is a bestselling author, playwright and motivational speaker. She started writing as a child, spending countless hours either reading or writing poetry, short stories, stage plays and novels. Vanessa's creative endeavors took on new meaning in 1994 when she became a Christian. Since then, her writing has been centered on themes of redemption, often focusing on characters facing multidimensional struggles.

Vanessa's novels have received rave reviews, with several appearing on *Essence* magazine's bestseller list. Miller's work has received numerous awards, including Best Christian Fiction Mahogany Award and a Red Rose Award for Excellence in Christian Fiction. Miller graduated from Capital University with a degree in organizational communication. She is an ordained minister in her church, explaining, "God has called me to minister to readers and to help them rediscover their place with the Lord."

She is currently working on a She Who Finds a Husband trilogy.